THE HOTEL

DAISY JOHNSON

JONATHAN CAPE
LONDON

1 3 5 7 9 10 8 6 4 2

Jonathan Cape, an imprint of Vintage, is part of the
Penguin Random House group of companies whose addresses
can be found at global.penguinrandomhouse.com

First published by Jonathan Cape in 2024

Copyright © Daisy Johnson 2024

Daisy Johnson has asserted her right to be identified as the author of this
Work in accordance with the Copyright, Designs and Patents Act 1988

These stories were originally commissioned by and
broadcast on BBC Radio 4.

penguin.co.uk/vintage

Typeset in 10.4/15pt Palatino LT Pro by Jouve (UK), Milton Keynes
Printed and bound in Great Britain by Clays Ltd, Elcograf S.p.A.

The authorised representative in the EEA is Penguin Random House Ireland,
Morrison Chambers, 32 Nassau Street, Dublin D02 YH68

A CIP catalogue record for this book is available from the British Library

ISBN 9781787335264

Penguin Random House is committed to a sustainable future
for our business, our readers and our planet. This book is made
from Forest Stewardship Council® certified paper.

FOR TC

Contents

The Hotel	1
The Witch	11
The Build	21
Infestation	31
Clean	41
The Wedding	51
Conference	61
The Monster	71
Night Watch	81
Briony	91
Haunted	101
Mother	111
The Story	121
The Priest	131
The Film	141
Acknowledgements	151

THE HOTEL

This is what we know about The Hotel:

> It is bigger on the inside than the outside.
> Do not go into Room 63.
> Doors and windows do not stay in the same places.
> The Hotel listens when you speak.
> The Hotel watches.
> The Hotel knows everything about you.
> The Hotel knew you before you arrived.
> The Hotel looks different to different people.
> We'll be at The Hotel soon.
> The Hotel is familiar.
> The Hotel is a stranger in an alley.

It is difficult to find information about The Hotel online and a degree of patience is needed. The language used to write about The Hotel is difficult, tangled. Websites spring up rife with stories and soon become pitted with absences, sentences which begin and end nowhere, vanishing punctuation. In a book on haunted British buildings there is a chapter on The Hotel which is pulled before publication and never read by anyone. Photographs of The Hotel have a habit of going missing. But it is possible to hunt down small snippets of information, to trawl through history for the signs.

Before The Hotel there is a farm on the land. A small building that cannot have had more than a few chickens, perhaps some pigs. The death records from the area show that no one lives for long at the property, that there is a plague of unfortunate accidents and stillbirths. The farm is passed down through a family whose misfortunes must have felt weighty. Before the fire which destroys the farm and the sale of the land which leads to the building of The Hotel, a woman lives on the property – the wife of a descendant – and dies there also. The woman seems to be notorious in the surrounding area as someone who has some talent in prediction and who the neighbours are suspicious of. At this time a spate of child deaths is recorded which can now be attributed to farm run-off into the water supplies, but at the time is blamed on the woman. The woman is childless and her family are not originally from the country, and this makes her a suspect and leads to her being drowned in the pond out the back of the farm. Before drowning she scratches some words into the front door of the house. The words read: I WILL SEE YOU SOON.

The Hotel exhibits what might be described as personality traits. It seems to know the people who come and go within its walls. Perhaps more insidiously The Hotel seems to collect people to it, has a magnetism that is sometimes

The Hotel

impossible to ignore. The curse that follows The Hotel might be blamed entirely on the unnamed woman who was killed there, but it seems more likely that any unfortune comes in fact from the earth itself and she was only the first person to note it.

The Hotel build is rife with issue and for a long time it looks like it may remain unfinished. The ground is sodden and swallows the foundations; there are accidents when scaffolding fails. Trees that are dug up on one day reassert themselves over the weekend. Still. It is done, the building is finished in 1919. The style is Gothic Revival; long chimneys, narrow windows covered with hood mouldings, stained glass which dims the light, an orchard. This is where everything begins.

In the 1950s a poet better known for her meandering nature poems writes a few lines about The Hotel, embedded in a longer, strange piece about a lost love and a failed suicide attempt. In the poem The Hotel is transitory, almost mythic, a dangerous place which reappears throughout history in different guises. A year later the poet succeeds where before she failed and is drowned in the sea off the North Norfolk coast. In the boarding house where she was staying is a notebook with scraps of writing, some scrawled images in pen the most distinctive of which seem to be of The Hotel, recognisable by its severe chimneys. Beneath the drawings the poet has written: I WILL BE THERE SOON.

*

In the early 1990s there is a series of accidents at or near The Hotel. The girlfriend of a relatively well-known married politician is found locked inside one of the rooms, starving, wild-eyed. A group of schoolchildren who are camping in the local forest get lost and, when they are found, appear to have lost the ability to speak or understand language. More smaller incidents abound: room keys become embedded in the flesh of hands, people working in the hotel fall down the stairs or end up locked in the lifts. For a year The Hotel is closed for renovations, and when it opens up again there is a time where nothing is recorded. The Hotel is no longer the haunt of the upper classes but becomes popular for weddings and anniversaries, for work conferences.

The Hotel seems to be seasonal, sometimes cyclical in that years can go by with relative peace and then there is disturbance. It is not clear if these occasions are brought on by any outside events, if The Hotel is sensitive to changes in government or peace, to rising temperatures or local badger culling.

What does seem clear is that The Hotel does not affect everyone in the same way. For some it is possible to visit and see nothing out of the ordinary. The Hotel is not far from Cambridge or the sea on the train. In the winter there are big fires in the bar and the rooms are warm, dressing gowns hang from the backs of the bathroom doors. The newspapers are left outside the doors in the morning and it is possible to order breakfast in bed, the bright orange yolks from a farm

The Hotel

down the road. There are oysters, fresh that day. Sometimes there are small surprises on a pillow: chocolate, an apple from the trees in the garden. A review online says: I really needed a break and the hotel was perfect, I am so rested, I am so much calmer. A review online says: I saw her for the first time since she died and she looked the same. The soap at the hotel is made at a Cotswold lavender farm and the coffee is Fairtrade and good with milk from a local dairy herd. A review online says: Next time we are asking for Room 63. For some it is possible to visit and come away contented, looking forward to returning. For others it is not this way. It is difficult to pin down exactly what type of person will visit The Hotel and see it for what it is. Often they are solitary, separated from their families or preferring to live alone, troubled by social situations, nervous in crowds. Many drink too much or find it difficult to sleep, have obsessive tendencies. Some find it hard to let go. Still there are those who do not drink, who come with their family or friends, who enjoy crowded rooms and long phone conversations, and they too will hear how the TVs in The Hotel sometimes speak to one another and the windows move in the night.

It is not possible with any certainty to go to The Hotel and feel safe. It is not wise to ever do so.

It is hard to say why people come to The Hotel despite most knowing the mythology surrounding it. The Hotel is listed as one of the most haunted buildings in Britain; accounts of activity at The Hotel are widespread. For many this alone is reason enough to visit – out of morbid curiosity or disbelief – but for some, those who work and live near The Hotel, there is always the question of why. Why don't they leave? Why do they often return again and again to a place that is clearly not only unsettling but, for some, dangerous? This question can only be posed by those who have not visited The Hotel. To go there, even once, is to feel something that might be akin to a tidal pull. Not only is it difficult not to return physically after a prior visit, it is also seemingly hard to stop the mind wandering towards that building, tall and grey on the dark fen land.

In 2016 The Hotel sits closed for three years. Though there are occasional interested buyers, The Hotel's reputation precedes itself and no sale goes through. Nature reasserts quickly. Ivy breaks in through the windows and grows amok across the ceilings, down through the rotting floors. Mice breed in the walls. In the summer teenagers break in and make fires in the dark rooms; in the winter sometimes the homeless set up tents in the garden or make nervous forays inside to look for somewhere dry. Sometimes stray dogs or cats get in and become trapped, emerge all tooth. Occasionally there are forays from groups interested in the occult or stray couples looking for a thrill.

In 2019 The Hotel is burned to the ground. The flames can be seen from the motorway. By the time the fire engines get

The Hotel

close enough the building is gutted. In the grounds of The Hotel, buried beneath a cluster of willow trees, a film camera is found. The footage is partly destroyed but it appears to show a group of student film-makers who broke into the building the week before it was destroyed. The students are yet to be found and the footage on the camera is inconclusive, ending abruptly so it is not apparent whether they began the fire or have any knowledge of who did. The students in the film are excitable, at times we can hear their voices calling to one another or addressing the viewer. As they progress through The Hotel the film appears to break down and what we see becomes unclear. Towards the end there are images from a particular room, the white walls damp and sagging with mould. In the bathroom, above the bath the camera holds for a couple of moments on some graffiti, a single phrase visible: I WILL BE THERE SOON.

It is nearly impossible to collate and logically place all the stories about The Hotel. To begin and then to find some sort of ending, a moment of catharsis. And in this beginning what to include? The dreams a woman living a hundred miles from The Hotel had of walking around and around a tall building, opening doors only to find more doors. The drawings a small child in a Cornish nursery did of a red door with the number 63 written on it. The email a woman wrote to her son the day before she died in which she said, repeatedly: I will be there soon, I will be there soon. The cathedral in Ely which occasionally reported sightings in the night of a mirage hotel room set before the altar, the bed made, the TV on.

And if a beginning is attempted and somehow made successful, where then is an ending found? Is it possible that The Hotel ceased when it burned down or is it not more likely that the land itself holds some forbidding sense of identity? What grows there now? Nothing. What doors are there in the ground? Many. And is it possible that even though The Hotel is gone there is still some days a flash of it, a startling after-image of a building, tall chimneys, open front door?

It is not yet the end. It is time, tentatively, for a start. Fourteen stories of The Hotel in the fens.

THE WITCH

My husband brought me to this farmhouse to be his wife and though I was not born here this is where I will die.

My name is Mary Southgraves and I am ordinary in most every way, except that since I was a child I have had some talent at seeing what is ahead. This uncanny knowledge frightened my mother and angered my father and I became clever at keeping it to myself. These truths come to me in dreams or in the strong daylight they are spoken out loud into my head or put fully in words into my mouth. By the time I was a married woman and came here to this flat place I had learned how to be silent, and my husband did not know that I could see the milk curdle before it did or know when the old farm cat would die and how. I would keep quiet if I could but this land increases a power which was only ever small and insignificant and makes it large, and this farmhouse sits like a sullen demon upon it and draws the knowledge from me. I am wilful here and find myself wild; worse, I find the knowing comes so strongly that it lays time flat and it is near impossible to tell the present from the future.

*

THE HOTEL

In describing the farmhouse to me my husband grew it larger and grander than it is, added on rooms, created warmth where there is nothing but cold stone. There is a kitchen with a fire that smokes and a wooden table with one leg shorter than the others. There is a windowless bedroom, which in the winter months we share with the chickens. Off the kitchen is a scullery, a place that I do not go. This is the extent of my prison, and beyond the windows the fens, great dark fields, the barn where the pigs live, the pond where I will die.

My husband is a kind man but in the last months he has become afraid of me, and I know he goes and speaks to the other men, farmers all, about this fear. I cannot help telling him of what I see, of the small mistakes he will make that will lead to the desolation of this farm, of the sadness that will rule his life. I cannot help also speaking the truth to the women who sometimes come by looking for gossip or free eggs, who have started keeping their distance and treating me with a wary dislike. I know they speak of me in the village and sometimes send their children around to pull my drying sheets into the mud on wash day. They are sharp-tongued, but it does not stop them coming to me when they are with child or cannot sleep or grow so tired with fear and want only to know; whether that knowing will bring them peace or only despair. They come in the night, without light, and scrape their fingernails against the kitchen window and I speak to them, faceless, in the dark and they leave flour or sacks of potatoes as payment.

The Witch

And in the day, they turn their faces away from me, speak my name loudly.

For a time my husband and I carried love between us, so carefully, like a basket of eggs. When it was jostled he would straighten it and I would move my hip to keep us even, to give us happiness. We held this love at times in our hands and felt it warm our palms and I thought of his softly dimpled cheeks, the rough pads of his thumbs. The farmhouse appeared on the flats ahead of us and he held my cheek and spoke of children and of long years and seeing it coming. I knew that we would have none of these and that the ground beneath the farm was ill with hatred. My husband led me around the building with great pride and when we came to the scullery I felt a fear I had never felt before, a mighty wave which silenced my voice. The scullery is a small room with shelves for jam, the floor is dirt and there is often some disturbance there; moles which dig up and leave mounds of earth. My husband said joyfully that when his mother had lived on the farm she once filled the shelves with 63 jars of preserved fruits and vegetables, an enormous amount, and the number rang through me and hurt my gums, and I saw every one of those 63 jars smashed to the floor and my husband's mother's wrists torn as if bitten by the glass. Ever after I have thought of that room as 63 and I will not go in there. The number comes to me in the night and I have to muffle my face against the pillow to stop myself from saying it out loud.

*

THE HOTEL

I do not know what it is about this land, but it has some hold. I always hoped in death I would return to the place I was born, but I know now that I will linger here, making the same steps I have made day by day in life. It is said that bodies do not rot in this earth but stay preserved, and perhaps that is why this place calls its dead to it. I will be there soon I think and I will see the reams of those who have gone before and who cluster in this small space like animals, pressing their flat faces to the world of the living. At times I long for it, though it is not peace and it is not quiet.

There is some sickness in the water which I dream about one night. The wells are stagnant and the rivers have carried a plague from upstream. I boil the well water and try to speak to my husband about the disease which will be especially cruel to the young and the very old. He lowers his head towards the table and eats his breakfast without looking at me, the way he has taken to doing when I speak about anything he does not believe in. I take a basket of bread and go to the other farmhouses which lie across the fields between here and the village. The children see me coming and go running with my name on their lips to their mothers, who stand with their legs braced on the ground and watch me until I am close. I offer them bread and they become civil, but when I speak of the sickness they anger and will not talk to me. I see the faces of the children who will die like bright stars. These women do not trust me because I have not been, and never will be, able to have a

The Witch

child, but their own children go now calmly to death and they do nothing.

What is in this land is some possessive quality, some unquietness. It is clear to me that there are places which have as much personality as any person or animal and this is one of them. This land and I share some similarities, this land knows the way I know, this land can see everything, it can see us and what lies ahead. I am afraid here and would like to leave but that is not what happens.

The first of the children falls sick and the news is heard all over. The sickness is bad and the child is dead by nightfall. We grieve this body that used to be someone's baby. We put it in the ground where, in a month, it will rise swollen to the surface. The mother comes in the deep of night to our house and slams her mourning flesh against our door and tries to call me out and my husband locks me in the scullery for protection. I sit in the scullery with my eyes closed and my hands over my ears and I hear the voice of my husband's dead mother counting those 63 jars and I wait for her to realise I am there.

There are many deaths and the graveyard is full. I am beset upon on the way to the village and beaten bloody. They try to take my tongue but I run from them and when I make it home my husband will not look at or speak to me. They think I have killed the children with my words and I cannot convince them otherwise. When I wake I am in the scullery again and there is the glint of glass in my hand which I have placed against my throat. There were 63 jars here and this is the room of 63 fears, all clamouring, all so loud. It is this room I will come back to and perhaps this room leads only into the ground.

Bad floods, and the bodies of the recently dead resurface. Our grief is enormous and overtakes us. The bodies have the countenance of those asleep, as if they have come back only to see us once more. Our barn is set afire.

When I wake one morning I find my husband gone. The present and the future are close friends now, clutching hands. The land has a sort of singing sound that comes from it and goes into me. I make bread to try to find some peace in the kneading but the loaf is sour and doesn't rise. I see the world of the dead coming towards me across the coal-black fields, I taste the water from the pond on my tongue. I want to leave some semblance of love, some piece of myself given in good faith. I take the bread knife and go to the front door and carve my name and my husband's name and my mother's name into the wood, these people I have tried to love. Except when I step back from the door, I have not written these words, I have been deceived, I have written instead: I WILL SEE YOU SOON. I know that these words mean that I was right and I will come back and I will linger here.

I see the farmers coming. They come from all directions thinking to close off any escape but I will not try to run. I

The Witch

wish that my husband was here so I could tell him I am sorry, that I still carry that basket of eggs carefully, even if he no longer carries it with me. They take me by the arms and by the hair and we go as a monstrous form all together towards the pond. I am lifted from my feet which drag, I am pulled forward. As we go I catch something that might be a glimpse of a future beyond my own, a heady image, so far from me that it is shadowed. There is another building in the place where the farmhouse once stood, a tall building with long chimneys and such watchful windows. We are at the pond now and the vision dissolves as I am thrust forward and into the water. There is mud in my mouth and covering my eyes; I cannot see my own hands. At the bottom of the pond there is a door and I find myself in possession of a heavy bunch of keys to open it and I slip from myself and go through the door and close it behind me.

THE BUILD

I have a job building a new hotel out on the fens. The news in the town is that the build is already souring and tainted with bad luck, the money is good for nothing. Many of the men are giving it a wide berth and so they are left with a ragtag crew: the one-armed man, the teenage twins, drunks, secret keepers, loners, and me; a woman who needs the money so badly she has no other choice.

I have never been to the fens before. I am surprised by the colour of the earth which looks as if darkness itself has slipped from the sky and filled the ground. I was born in Yorkshire and this place of no-hills seems ill to me, so flat, the canals like blood-carrying arteries dug down. I catch a glimpse of plans for The Hotel and, yes, it will be magnificent, in the Gothic style, fit for all sorts. It is impossible to imagine it now. The rain comes down in sheets and the old pond overflows; we are drenched, our boots are sodden. We are clearing the ground, preparing it for the foundations. We work hunched, protecting our faces. The foreman bemoans there being a woman on the build but we all look the same in the rain and the mud and I work hard and do not speak. I have strong arms, I will show them with my arms that I am good for this.

The ground is covered in scrub, and trees with such thick roots it feels like murder as we heave them up. The pond will need to be drained and covered over. It is a slick, miserable place; slimy rocks, no fish, only the oily water and the reeds sharp enough to cut skin. The money men come in their cars to see the work although there is nothing to see yet. They shelter beneath umbrellas and do not speak to us. We are swamp monsters and already one of the men has left, calling it an impossible task and the money too poor for the job. The rest of us work harder, each with our own reason to need to be here and not in the warmth.

We camp on slightly higher ground but still the rain comes in through the bottom of the tents and I wake soaked. I can hear the teenage twins murmuring to one another. They are runaways I think, their eyes are always swivelling as if they can see through the backs of their heads. In the night there is some disturbance, a shout and then the sound of the wind and then a low moan of fear. In the morning the one-armed man says he saw a floating light by the pond when he went to relieve himself, a light that bobbed above the ground but seemed to have no structure holding it up. The one-armed man is kinder to me than the rest and I listen while he speaks but the others spit and jeer and it is decided the man had only a nightmare.

*

The Build

I work without speaking, work faster and better than the others, who complain of trench foot. The foreman notes my work, I see him looking. I dig the trees up and cut them for the wood that will one day burn in The Hotel's big fireplaces and keep the guests warm. The foreman calls me to the shack and touches my breast under my clothes and we stand awkwardly and then I go back to work. Little progress seems to be made. We slog through the weather. We wade in water to the calf.

Again, trouble in the night. I hear the one-armed man shouting and the teenage twins answering in raised, fearful voices and then I am out in the darkness, stumbling around. Everyone has come out of their tents and we collide and fall, and in the distance I think I see a sharp light, raised from the ground. There is a great dispute and a fight nearly breaks out. The one-armed man is drunk perhaps, his forehead when I touch it is clammy with sweat and he slurs his words. When the foreman comes in the morning five of the more superstitious men have left already, forgoing their pay. I work beside the one-armed man and he tells me not to go near the pond but will not say more when I ask. We work hard that day, all of us driven onwards and silent in our toil, and by dark the ground is cleared and only the pond remains. We must drain it and then cover it and then lay the foundations. The concrete will come in a week and we must be ready for it.

*

The machinery brought in to drain the pond breaks and will not be fixed and the replaced machine goes the same way. The foreman grows seething with rage. Another machine brought in to no avail. The one-armed man watches and I watch him. He has the reflection in his eyes of whatever he saw that night which has made him sick, his fingers curled. The teenage twins who were once chattery as birds are silent and wan. I try to raise their spirits. I do not believe in ghosts or fate. Later I will come to regret this and know that I should have left when I could. We tell jokes to keep up the mood and even the one-armed man cracks a smile.

There is an argument. We are to go into the pond – it is not deep they say – and bail it out with buckets. We are to use our bodies as machines. They bring waders for us to wear but many of the men will not go into the water. They have seen the light, they say, and they have heard the words that sometimes come from the pond, voices which say their name and seem to know them. I have not heard this and I cannot be certain I saw the light. I take a bucket and I go in with the teenage twins who will do anything they are told, like frightened dogs. It is a thankless, impossible task. I stand at the deepest extent of the pond, near covered to my chin, and send the water in buckets back to the shore where they are emptied. It is impossible while here not to dream of drowning or of those who might have drowned before. I feel myself womanly in the water in a way I am rarely certain of and I know that when we drown we are all the same.

*

The Build

Another disturbed night. We need the sleep but the sleep will not be given to us. I hold the one-armed man in my arms and his eyes look over my shoulder and seem to see something there. The teenage twins huddle and stare and whisper to one another. When the light of morning comes there is some relief, coffee, hot eggs. The other men are beginning to hate the one-armed man, they are afraid and they use their fear like knives and sharp tools. We run on desperation alone. The one-armed man puts his mouth close to my ear and tells me he saw a woman by the pond last night, holding a lantern and looking at him. The dead come back here, the one-armed man says, I think we will come back here too.

We work for a long time and do not stop to rest. The pond fights us and we bail like sailors in a sinking boat. Word spreads of what the one-armed man saw and I see some of the others looking at me mistrustfully. They think I was the woman by the water, perhaps; they do not like me. Even the teenage twins who I have become friendly with keep their distance. At lunch the foreman does not take me into his shack as has been his way and for this at least I am relieved. How much I would like to give away this pressure of womanhood, these heavy bags which I carry uphill and would like to put down even for a moment. My arms are strong but when I lose my balance in the pond and fall beneath the surface I feel, just for a moment, someone holding me down.

*

THE HOTEL

There is a lightness to the evening. Someone has found fireworks and they go up into the sky in red and blue sparks and fall back towards us and one of the men sets his beard on fire and there is something like laughter. A relief. The teenage twins have a strange dance they do for us, they bop and swing around with linked arms and then fall in a heap and leap up and do it again. The one-armed man sings a song and tells rude limericks that have us all howling and it is easy then to forget our watery despair.

Oh, well, dreams like ponds which are not shallow but go down a long way, caves really, and which I am swimming or falling through. In the way of dreams, I know more than I should and I understand that I should not stay here, that I must go, that this place is sick and that if I stay longer I will never be able to leave. In the way of dreams I see something which might be the future, or one of them, and The Hotel has a wide toothy smile and a clever mind like a child grown old. In the dream I tell myself that I must remember this urge to go, and do it in the morning without delay, but when I wake the dream is just a dream and I need money as much as I did before.

Another day and we make good progress. The pond is emptying out and we find old memories at the bottom: shoes, keys, farming tools. We bail quickly, passing the buckets, dreaming of concrete foundations. My next bucket is heavy and when I lift it, I see the gleam of white through the muck, and a word is passed between us as the bucket goes to land, so

The Build

that by the time it is emptied we all know that I have brought up bones. I hear someone saying my name, sowing discord, but when I look none of the men are speaking.

We line the hole where the pond was and then fill it with dirt. Things are moving apace now; the new concrete is here. We are relieved and we laugh and touch one another's hands.

We forget to be afraid of the night, which comes like a blanket. There are the sounds of screams and shouts, someone lifts my tent and tears it clean from the ground and someone says in my ear: You must not build here. They are shouting that there is a woman going among them and then I am lifted and carried and they are pulling at my arms and legs and all of a sudden I remember how certain I was in the dream that I had to go. They are saying my name like a curse and their fists are falling on my face and stomach. I see the teenage twins dropping great blows upon me and the one-armed man snarling down his anger and in the darkness that lies ahead of me I see the shape of a building with tall chimneys.

INFESTATION

A small girl takes the branch of an apple tree that grows in the grounds of a hotel between both hands and shakes it back and forth, back and forth. It is 1968, the summer. Her parents are nearby on the lawn, reading the newspaper, drinking coffee. The girl's jaw shudders and the tree groans and the branch breaks free.

There is an infestation in one of the walls of The Hotel's laundry room. The girl watches the people, alien contraptions, masks. She trails after them, smells them, thinks of asking them what bugs but does not.

She is so fussy. In The Hotel's dining room she eats toast and potatoes but won't go near the buffet which strains heavily, a plethora of colour. The first night her mother brought experimental titbits over for her and she was nearly wild with the panic of seeing them, the grotesque pink seafood, the strangled pieces of meat. After that they don't bother and mostly she goes unnoticed, watching fascinated at how much everyone eats. After dinner her mother takes her upstairs and reads half a story and then kisses her forehead and goes back down. Cocktail hour, the girl says, cocktail hour.

She tries to stay in bed as instructed, but it's so hot and the duvet is tucked in on three sides and though she attempts counting sheep – also as instructed – they are all different colours, fanged, winged, distracting.

As an apology for the disturbance of the men in suits and masks, they are given free paper lanterns which are lit at twilight and go up into the darkening sky and away.

The third night she wrestles free, clucking. Roams the room, making small disturbances in the lines of toiletries in the bathroom. The light through the spyhole in the door criss-crosses over her feet. She broaches the corridor. It is blindingly light and the doors are all painted different colours, the walls red. She roly-polies up and down, lifting off from the balls of her feet, head over heels in a tangle of skirt. She tries the handles of doors – delicious fear – and some are closed to begin with but then clunk open, as if unlocked from the other side. Everyone is at cocktail hour or sometimes asleep, not noticing her as she inches in, hands fisted at her mouth.

The next day she is so tired, dead on her feet. Dead on my feet, she says out loud, deadonmyfeet. The men are there again with their plastic suits, the spray tanks, the shoe coverings they strip, laughing, off their feet after they are done. She imagines them climbing in and out of a man-sized hole

Infestation

in the wall, dropping in and down, holding their breath. She lounges and lolls on the grass and is told off by her mother who wants to know why she's so tired when she's done nothing all day?

The next night her parents linger in the room, smoking on the balcony, putting on lipstick. She feigns sleep, wants them badly to leave. The air stinks of cigarettes and perfume, the tiny bottle of gin that gets smashed on the bathroom floor. They parade in front of the mirror, seeming almost to leave and then becoming distracted again, looking for the room key, for the purse. Finally, they are gone. She rushes up and down the corridor, wild with freedom. Flops belly down onto the carpet and then looks up; voices from the stairwell. Her room, too far away to reach, the numbers on the doors swimming together. The voices sound like her parents' but then every adult sounds like them, conspiratorial, dull. She makes for the nearest door which seems to clunk unlocked as she approaches – like magic she thinks – compresses the handle, goes inside. Crouches and closes her eyes and waits. The voices come along the corridor and then go past and are silenced. When she opens her eyes there is someone there, in the bed, sat up, a splay of hair, looping eyes, small hands clutching the duvet. Hello? the girl says, thinking perhaps that she has somehow found herself, or at least a more obedient version, still asleep, doing as she's told. The other figure stares and then says, who are you?

*

Her name is Shirley. They reconvene the next day in the garden, suspicious, staining their white dresses green. The girl can feel her parents – hung-over – watching. Shirley has a pair of heavy binoculars around her neck and when the girl asks who her parents are, she gestures vaguely, encompassing the groups of many adults, preening on the lawn chairs, unfolding their newspapers. The girl feels the same way. They try one another out. Shirley pulls the girl's hair and the girl puts an earthworm in the pocket of Shirley's dress and they train the binoculars on one another's faces, looking for weakness. They climb one of the apple trees, skinning knees, grappling, and then fall together and stare at one another, waiting to see who will wail first. Neither does. At lunch they sit in silence at their separate tables and eat nothing and are mostly ignored. The girl says to her mother, Shirley says she hates her parents. But her mother doesn't seem to hear her. The girl opens and closes her mouth and wonders if maybe Shirley isn't real after all, is only an imagined friend she has cleverly created to fill the boring hours. Or perhaps The Hotel has given her Shirley, with the same magic it uses to open the locked bedroom doors. She doesn't really care either way.

The day slips away. They enact dark business together, hiding under the tables in the empty dining room, slipping behind the bar and edging full bottles almost off the counter, stealing lemons to suck until their cheeks ache. They collect bounty in the soft folds of their skirts and bury it in the garden: keys from behind the reception desk, mints from the pocket of an older woman's coat when she leaves it on her chair, a necklace that might have belonged to either of their mothers.

That night after dinner when their parents have gone to the bar they dare one another into rooms, leave dirty footprints in the baths, wrap themselves in the curtains. In one room there is a woman asleep, blindfolded, mouth ajar. They stand either side of her.

The next day – so tired – Shirley seems a bit of a pain. They lie on the grass not talking and occasionally, from the corner of her eye, the girl sees Shirley moving, making little jerks or hiccups. The girl wants to tell Shirley to go and never come back but she doesn't know how. At lunch she eats handfuls of salty peanuts until her belly hurts and her mother grows angry and tells her there'll be no dinner if she doesn't buck up her ideas. Buckupherideas, buckupherideas. I'm bored, she replies, hoping that they will do something with her and she won't have to see Shirley again, but her mother only closes her eyes and says, only boring people are bored.

The men were gone but now they are back again, the infestation not yet solved. Shirley and the girl watch them with the binoculars, peer into the van they have brought which is filled with unfamiliar instruments, crackling plastic sheeting, grim-looking bottles of poison. I dare you to drink it, the girl says, and Shirley pretends to, holding up the bottle, pressing the closed lid to her mouth. She is good fun, she is a pain. When the men stop for lunch the girls creep into the downstairs room where the infestation is, a laundry room with rows of washing machines and the floor softly powdered with white. The hole in the wall is much smaller than the girl imagined, about the size of her or Shirley curled up small. They look inside. There are comb nests, crusted together, jammed in. Shirley puts both hands over her face and when the girl smells the damp of her own fingers she realises she is doing the same. The men have destroyed some of the nests but others are whole still. The girl says, I dare you to touch them, but Shirley won't. I can't be your friend anymore, the girl says and Shirley stares at her, eyes like binoculars, fat-lipped.

For the rest of the day she keeps away from Shirley and haunts her parents, sitting grumpily at their feet in the garden, bringing them apples from the tree or good-shaped stones which they barely acknowledge. At dinner she gets in trouble for dropping her fork on the floor and then refusing to pick it up and is taken to bed early. A story, she asks piteously from beneath the starched duvet, but her mother says stories are for good girls and refuses. She lies enraged and kicking in the bed, pulling her own hair. She imagines Shirley at dinner, polite, eating her food.

Downstairs in the laundry room the men have left some of their equipment behind and have also carried down bricks to close up the space in the wall. The laundry machines look like folded-over women in white dresses with button dials.

Infestation

Shirley is already there, lingering in the dark, odd corners. They grab at one another's arms and bellies, pinching, pulling at the flesh, waiting for someone to beg out. The girl has stones from the garden in her pockets and her teeth are grimy with unspat toothpaste. Shirley is spotless, wet-haired, her nostrils pink and clean. The girl takes a stone in each hand, hides her hands in her pockets, then draws out her hands and holds them in front of her, closed. The stones feel so smooth they might almost not be there. If you pick the hand with the stone, the girl says, you go in the wall. Shirley seems defiant, uncaring. Her body smells of buffet food, mounds and mounds of it. Shirley touches one of the girl's hands and they look together at the stone laid out on the palm. The girl wants to take it back or show Shirley that she has cheated, there is a stone in both hands, there was no way of winning the game. She does not know how to stop something once it has started happening. The hole in the wall is the shape of a large cat sleeping. Shirley folds herself forward, tucks her arms in, fits inside the wall easily although she has to keep her body uncomfortably curled up, her knees to her chin. Her face inside the wall looks different: familiar, round, loosened. The girl picks up bricks from the floor and lays them on top of the bricks already there and gradually Shirley shrinks from sight, the sound of the cocktail hour going on above, the moment – here and here and here – where it could be put to an end but is not. The bricks are heavy and the girl's arms hurt and she thinks about this pain so intensely that she is surprised when there is only space for one more brick – Shirley's eye through the gap, open wide – and then there is no space at all.

In the morning her mother is in a good mood and coats the girl's eyelids with blue eyeshadow, says they will play games all day. The girl waits for Shirley to be found or for Shirley's parents to reveal themselves in a fury. Everyone is cracking open the tops of their boiled eggs. Someone is laughing very loudly and though she looks to see who it is, she cannot tell where it is coming from.

CLEAN

My name is Grace and I work at The Hotel because I have no choice. My father is dying and though there is no love lost between us, I need to pay for his care home. I wish I could leave this place but I don't think I will ever be able to.

On our days off we do Ouija boards in the empty rooms. Scarlet makes them with her daughters out of cut-up cereal boxes and a rubber stamp and we use a shot glass and ask questions about guests at The Hotel or about our own lives, our failing relationships, our intricate sorrows, the number of years we have left. Everyone knows that Ouija boards lie. Sometimes we lose count of the letters that come up and the messages are garbled, like lost words between radio stations or walkie-talkies. We lie on our bellies on the floors of the rooms and Jay circles our orders on the takeaway menu and then goes to pick them up. Sometimes we tell the Ouija board things instead of asking questions. It is good to know someone is listening. Scarlet tells stories about her daughters, who have quit school early and loll around the house or disappear for days, come back with briar-patch hair and torn tights. Jay tells stories about the things she finds under the beds or in the bathroom bins when the guests have left – these strange gifts – bags of sunflower seeds, a fancy fountain pen, once a goldfish in a plastic bag, which she took home and keeps in a bowl on her bedside table. I try not to tell the board anything although sometimes – full of spring rolls and Kung Pao fish – I slip up and find myself speaking to it. Mostly there isn't anything to tell but I talk about the online dates I've been on, the cold in the mornings when I wake up, what's on the news. I talk about my sister who's just got married and my sick father. We should be home. We are not working and we should not be here. We push our takeaway-stained plates under the bed even though it will be us – in just a few hours – who have to tidy them away. We get under the duvet and doze and sometimes in the quiet the shot glass moves of its own accord when we are nowhere near it and we cheer and call out questions, unable to see the answers.

The first week working at The Hotel I am unprepared although everyone in the local area has heard the stories. I haven't met Scarlet and Jay yet and I don't know the rules. Not the rules of the management but the rules of the building, which are different and change more often. A lot of the rules are: Pretend you didn't see that. Some of the rules are: Run, now. That first week I stink of fear-sweat and sometimes I open my mouth to scream and nothing comes out. The other cleaners watch me carefully and later I understand that they are watching for the moment I realise what I have got myself into. One morning all the radios on the different floors I am working on are talking to one another. It

Clean

takes me longer than it should to realise. On the first floor one says: Do you hear that, Sandra? And on the second floor a radio tuned to a different station says: Yes, I hear it, I hear everything. Another morning I go into a room on the third floor and there is something inside the mattress, moving, big as a body, elbows and knees pressing against the lining, working at the seams. I stand outside the door and when I get brave enough to go back in, whatever was there is gone. There are other things I could tell you but I won't. If I could work somewhere else I would, but this is the only job I even got an interview for.

There is a trolley I like best and make sure to get at the beginning of my shift. It has a slightly wonky wheel which means I can go slower than everyone else, taking my time, keeping an eye out. Sometimes The Hotel is just a hotel and the problems are just hotel problems. The way people leave their rooms when they check out, the stains in the bathrooms and on the white bed sheets, the way sometimes they don't leave and going in you find them drunk in the bath, the things people say to you.

Being here changes you. I can feel it changing me every day. Scarlet, who has worked here the longest, says that she's grown distracted over the years, never quite able to focus on anything. Sometimes at home I blink and I don't know how long I've been sat in the armchair, the TV is on but it isn't playing what I remember, my dinner is cold. When I first started working here and was less careful than I am now, I'd come home with parts of The Hotel in my skin, splinters of wood, small shards of metal. Once I woke in the night to a pain in the roof of my mouth and when I craned my head in the bright light of the bathroom mirror I could see something, long, sharp. I drew it out with tweezers. It was a nail, small and thin-tipped, a little rusty.

On our five-minute coffee and cigarette breaks (Jay's giving up but she comes and stands with us) sometimes we talk about how we will destroy The Hotel. It's a game we play. Scarlet always talks about fire, how she'd burn it down, starting in the kitchen and then going from room to room to make sure it took. Jay talks about diggers, bulldozers. I can never quite make myself say. I can never imagine it not being here.

There's a room none of us likes cleaning but someone has to do it so we take turns. Room 63. Things go missing in that room and it's no good putting down a bottle of bleach and walking away, because by the time you come back it'll be gone. As well as things going missing, sometimes things come back. I found a necklace in there that I lost when I was a child, something my father gave me as a bribe for silence and that I thought I'd left in the bin. Scarlet once found photos of her daughters in a frame, photos she doesn't remember taking. Jay won't talk about what she's found. The trick to cleaning the room is to do it quickly. I like to listen to music because the noises are the worst. You can't trust the sound here: the walls say your name, there are

Clean

footsteps close behind you but no one there when you turn. I leave the trolley outside the room and carry everything I need with me and don't put anything down or hesitate too long. There are guests who stay in the room over and over, who ask for it when they phone up to book. Sometimes you can recognise which ones they are, the ones who can't stop coming back. I've seen them getting out of their cars or taxis, seen them at reception. They are sickly looking; they have the look of addicts. Once in the lift, going down, a woman with wide eyes smiled at me, showing her teeth.

I know you, she said.

I didn't know what to say so I just stood there. There was no one else in the lift but us. I watched the numbers going, willing them faster. She smiled wider.

I know you.

I knew which room she was going to when she got off. She turned and watched me, smiling, through the closing doors.

Scarlet's been off sick for nearly two weeks now and we've all been picking up the slack. There aren't enough of us. I've called her a couple of times but no one ever picks up. Jay says she went round there but the curtains were drawn and she couldn't get an answer when she knocked. We try to share Room 63 between us, but it's been falling to me more and more. Jay says she can't go in there anymore, that she's been waking up in the night stood at her front door, dressed, holding her car keys, ready to come back here. I do the room as quickly as I can, nearly running, headphones in, whipping the sheets off the bed. Still, I can feel it for the rest of the day, like swallowing a bone, an internal pressure. Sometimes I find myself back there although I had been going somewhere else, my feet moving without my realising. I've started making mistakes in other places in The Hotel. I've been leaving messages in the steam in the bathrooms, on the mirrors and the shower doors. I keep writing: I WILL BE THERE SOON. I get in trouble with management for not cleaning properly but actually I think I am making new mess, smearing food across the beds, walking in dark clods of mud which stick to the carpet and stink.

My father dies in the night. The care home rings me and I go to pick up his things. I stand in the car park having a cigarette. I feel myself starting to cry but instead I laugh and laugh. My father was the worst person I have ever met and for years I was tied to him, an anchor wrapped around my waist. I know that I paid to care for him because I was under his control and that I am free now. I ring The Hotel and hand in my notice. I will find a job somewhere else. I will be homeless. I will not go back there. I go home and I sleep fourteen hours and when I wake up I am stood outside of The Hotel, waiting. The front door is hooked open and I see Jay watching me from a window. I go home again, shaking, but the next day I am back once more, my uniform on, the trolley waiting for me. I cannot leave.

On our day off Jay and I go to Room 63 and do the Ouija board. I think time might have passed without our being

Clean

able to hold on to it. There are the crumbs from fortune cookies and spring rolls on the floor and Jay's eyes are lifted to the ceiling as if in prayer. She has her finger on the shot glass but she is not watching the answers. I watch the glass spinning wildly, rising onto its edge, careering around. It says my name five times and then it says my father's name, the letters arranging and rearranging so fast they blur. Every hair on my body stands on end and the skin between each finger and toe is taut and trembling, I can taste soap in my mouth as if I have been swilling at the sink the way my father would sometimes make me do, trying to clean my throat. I heave myself up and walk unsteadily to the door, bent forward against a pressure which feels like wind. At the door I turn back to reach out to Jay but she is already gone.

THE WEDDING

The organisation of the hen do was not without stress or strife. The conversation took place over a six-month period and some weekends it was all I found myself doing; cross-checking hotels, trawling reviews and trying to quell the uprising of passive-aggressive arguments among the group. The maid of honour was set on Las Vegas and wouldn't be shouted down despite general worries about pricing. The bride's sister wanted to bring her two dogs. Arguments which began with discussions about cocktail bars spiralled into day-long debates about carbon offsetting and orange wine. I dreamed in lists and figures, long streams of numbers tallying up the costs of bike hire or life drawing classes. The bride, who wasn't in the message thread, started sending me annoyed voice notes; the bride's sister was crying down the phone. I rarely felt myself moved to anger. If anything I was mellow, too easily swayed by others' decisions. I had finished university and was living at home and I still hadn't managed to tell my parents that I didn't eat meat anymore, that I couldn't partake on steak and chip Fridays. The online messages about the hen party were getting worse, streams of almost vitriol, comments made about relatives on both sides of the bridal party. One Saturday I steeled my nerves and waded into an argument about hotels vs cottages which had turned nasty. I could hear the TV downstairs. The bride's sister was firing off emojis quicker than I felt possible. I didn't know what to do. It looked like maybe we would never make a decision. One of the bride's close friends sent a late-night email, tight with annoyance and finality: she had found a nice-looking hotel online and booked it for us all. This is where we were going, it was going to be great. There was an uneasy silence from the group and then begrudging agreement.

The bride and I used to dig up worms and feed them to one another, build dams. When she lost her virginity she rang me and screamed down the phone, a sound like a steam engine, and then cackled and I knew what had happened without her saying a word. We fell out of touch and I was surprised by the invitation to the hen do. I had never met her fiancé. I could remember what her face looked like when she ate worms. We were no longer the only two black girls in a Welsh village. We were no longer anything to one another. I remembered holding her hair back as she threw up into a toilet with a Harry Potter FLOO NETWORK sticker on it and then brushing her teeth for her. I remembered her holding my hands and kissing me with a certainty that drove words from me. I remembered us skipping along the side of a road in Wales, heading for nowhere. She wasn't heading for nowhere anymore; she was getting married.

*

The Wedding

We are organised to the teeth. There will be afternoon tea, a cocktail-making workshop, a trip to a nearby spa, a champagne picnic and a pottery class in the garden. The wedding will be nothing in comparison to this. The rest of the hen party gather early at The Hotel. We have penis balloons and sashes; photos of the bride pinned to our chests. The Hotel staff whisper around us, smiling, picking things up. The bride is late. The Hotel has such tall chimneys and smells of honeysuckle, so sweet it is almost unbearable. We stand out on the gravel drive and wait for her to arrive. I am sweating. I try to think what I will say to her, practise the words in my head. We once swam in the sea and she disappeared ahead of me, drowned I thought, and I ducked under and saw her swimming, eeling. She arrives in a taxi and we pull her into our arms, wailing our cheers. Someone is chanting: LAST NIGHT OF FREEDOM, LAST NIGHT OF FREEDOM. Although the wedding isn't for months. She looks the same as she did when we were teenagers, a little embarrassed. I wait for her eyes to find mine but they skate over me, like slipping on ice.

The days pass quickly. We are so loud that it is difficult to hear the words we say. We make lewd pottery and snicker jokes about the wedding night. We get so drunk we stumble and cackle and hold one another up. In the mornings we are a little sombre and the bride stays in her room until lunch. I am sharing a bed with the bride's sister who snores and talks in her sleep, long rambling sentences about tax audits and the price of petrol. Sometimes I think I see the bride looking at me carefully, studying my face, but when I turn she isn't even there. There are things I want to say to her which weigh in my stomach and give me indigestion, stop me from sleeping.

One night I get up and leave the room. It is three o'clock in the morning and everything is quiet, the automatic lights flashing on to long corridors, red carpets, the open lift doors. I pad barefoot down to the reception desk which is empty, the reflection of my tatty white nightie in the long windows. I want a drink or a cup of tea, something to eat. Behind me something moves, a doubling reflection, and when I turn the bride is there, watching me carefully. She has her hair covered and without make-up she looks so young I feel confused, as if time has cheated on us. I remember the taste of her mouth and she smiles as if she knows what I am thinking. We go into the bar together and raid the herbal tea selection, sit on the tall bar stools watching each other's faces in the long mirror behind the bottles. We don't say anything and at the same time we dare one another silently to speak. It is the first time all week I've been alone with her. I wonder what her husband looks like, whether he can speak Welsh the way she does, whether he knows the taste of the sea. She lifts her tea cup from the bar and presses it to her mouth. In the mirror she looks like a ghost, a little blurred, and me blurred also beside her. I open my mouth to ask her if this is real and she holds my hand on the bar to silence me. Her fingers are dusty and rough. She opens her lips and

The Wedding

smiles at me and there is something wrong with her teeth, they look like bricks set into her gums.

In the day I wait for the bride to mention our night-time meeting but she barely even speaks to me. There is a salsa class and we whirl around the room, off the beat, knocking hips. I want her so badly I can't find the way out. I want there to be a flashing exit door to escape from this feeling, I want every fire alarm in the building to go off at once.

The next night when I get to the bar she is already there, her back to me. Her neck is very long like the banister of a staircase and her fingers lie on the wood like keys. When she speaks her voice is gravelly, not quite the way I remember it. She tells me about The Hotel, the long history, the hauntings that have taken place here. The Hotel knows everyone, she says. She takes my hand and we walk out of the bar and into the reception area. I can feel something thrumming between our clasped hands, like a bell struck and ringing. I wonder if I went upstairs into the bride's room whether I would find her asleep there, eye mask on, oblivious to the fact that here I was, clinging on to her cold-fingered double. We go behind the reception desk and touch the hanging keys, their small mouths and little jagged teeth. There is a door behind the desk and she opens it, smiling at me, and we go inside. Her face is not quite right and I have the sense that, when I close my eyes, something slips from her and she is uncovered in a way I am not ready to see. She puts her hands on me. I think of us the way we were when we were younger and the possibility of love hung between us like fireflies on a dark night. I can barely breathe.

On the final night of the hen party the bride weeps and gathers us into her arms, clings to us. Her make-up is smudged by tears and snot and we wail together in mourning, wrapping our limbs around one another, rocking our bodies. A penis-shaped balloon pops and makes us all yell louder, as if marriage is a small death and this the walk to the gallows. I press my face to the bride's neck and she pulls back and looks at me quizzically, wrinkling her nose. I see the meanness flash in her eyes a moment before she speaks. We kissed when we were teenagers, she announces to the group, and they pull back and stare at us. We kissed and she still loves me. The bride's sister lets out a little hushed moan of shock, shakes her head, whispers, but she's getting married. I shouldn't have invited you, the bride says simply, squeezing my hand regretfully, you have to let go. My face is burning, they draw themselves away from me, moving their arms so our skin doesn't touch, letting out their breath in uncomfortable gasps.

I find my bride waiting for me that night. I have always felt myself a lock and she comes to me in the shape of a key, hard-handed, devastating. She does not have any luggage with her although when she moves her pockets clink together, as if she has filled them with pieces of metal. We stand together at the front door. I turn to look at her and

The Wedding

when she looks back for a moment she is not human at all but brick and stone and thin arrow-shaped windows. When I blink she has once more the face of the person I have loved since I was a child and it is good enough or it is better than that. I wonder if she will survive leaving the building and I hold her around the middle thinking to keep her together, stop her from turning entirely to dust in my arms. She shakes me away and runs ahead, flashing through the trees. We go to the road and then walk and walk, now going together, now drifting apart, like skaters. At the nearest town we stop for breakfast. We eat sausages and eggs, plateful after plateful of toast slathered in butter. She speaks quickly to me, mouth full, famished, of our life together, of all the years we have, of all the fear that is to come. I hold her and tell her I love her and she tells me she knows.

CONFERENCE

I got the job straight out of university. I was lucky. I didn't know anyone in the city but it didn't matter. There was a big bar on the ground floor of the office and my first night there was a mixer for all the new people like me. Everything was free, endless drinks and no food and we all got really drunk but it was fine, there were dormitories in the basement. I slept there a lot that first year. In the morning I had an enormous hangover and I was embarrassed and felt stupid. But everyone was hung-over or said they were and there was a big breakfast that we could have whatever we wanted from and the secretaries kept ferrying in fresh coffee and Red Bull. Everything was so big and loud and the way they talked about it, everything was GREAT and FANTASTIC and they kept talking about OPPORTUNITIES and ROOM FOR GROWTH. Nothing was specific but everything was pitched at an excited level, just above my understanding. I photocopied things so fast they were a blur. There was a meeting about a possible meeting and I wrote things down and then typed them up and there were emails about possible meetings about possible other meetings. Lunch was on the top floor, there was a man in a chef's uniform making burgers to order, most of them blue or rare, and a pancake-making station. Blood from the burger ran like water down the inside of my wrist.

Even then I think I saw them. Out of the corner of my eye or when I turned quickly. Sometimes in the enormous, mirror-filled lifts there would be a slight burnish to the reflection, like hands on my shoulders or around my mouth. This was the early sense of them, as not one form but many, like the birds which amassed above the office on windy days.

I was excited to be there. I didn't want to be anywhere else. I often fell asleep at my desk with my head on my arms. I drank what everyone else drank at the bar: champagne, freezing-cold chugs of lager. I longed for one of the big offices we were all aiming for with their glass eyes looking over the city. There was a constant flow and rush and you were in or out. The lights never switched off, the coffee stations at every corner were always manned. Sometimes we pulled all-nighters in a way I never would have at university, comrades in arms, firing questions around the room. These nights were the best, the city darkening around us, the bottles we cracked open at three in the morning, our hands moving on the keys with a frantic energy I felt in my gut.

I forgot to phone my mum for months at a time. On New Year's Eve, wishing in the year 2015, I had five missed calls from her but we were partying all night and I kept forgetting to ring back. When we eventually spoke she said, but what

Conference

do you actually do there? I felt the words before I said them, greasy with freshly cooked burger fat, slick with expensive hand soap. We make things happen.

There were small moments, uncomfortably gendered. Sometimes when I walked into a meeting ready to give a presentation I'd spent two days preparing, one of the older men who came and went from the office would ask me to get everyone coffee, and, unable to find the words, I would go do it. By the time I came back the meeting would have moved on and no one would have noticed the presentation hadn't happened. These older men swam in and out, and each time the shoal was disturbed, a shudder running through us, the order displaced. We knew the smell of their aftershave, and the way they took their coffee was so embedded in my brain that sometimes I woke up saying it out loud. From behind they were almost indistinguishable from one another but from the front the sharpness of this one's face or the upturned smile of that one separated them. I grew to like the nauseating fear that they instilled, the panic that burned for longer than they were there, fuelling us. Of course, also, they were handsy, overly friendly, familiar in a way that suggested they remembered what we'd worn last time but not our names.

I was sent out by one to buy a present for his wife once, something sexy. I trawled shops in Soho, came back with leather. He was discussing a proposal with one of my male counterparts and when I came in he looked up and seemed to somehow see the wall behind me, as if my form was pocked with small viewing holes. He'd changed his mind, he said, he didn't want to give it to his wife, he wanted to give it to me. I felt water building through me, the sudden seizure of a torrent reaching a weir. In the office bar that night I drank steadily, the clear liquid running down my chin. My male counterpart – who'd been in the room when it had happened – came over and spoke slowly to me, touched my hips and bottom, as if now finally he understood the roles. We had been almost friends before but there was a new slickness between us, as of cold custard or car oil.

The conference was an important time of the year. One of the other people on my team who'd been there before said The Hotel was reported to be haunted and that's why we always went there, sometimes there were themed evenings where we dressed as ghosts or vampires. There were lectures and chaired discussions and at night we congregated in the bar. The bosses went and played golf at a nearby course in the day, but in the evenings they appeared in our midst, foxes in the chicken coop. The memories from the night were often hazy, like repeatedly driving into fog.

One of the bosses had a casual air to him, came to the bar without a tie or a jacket, would buy rounds of drinks for everyone, make jokes. In the corridor after a long night, I was hunting for my room when I found him, or he found me. God he was drunk he said, although something about his face made me wonder. It was true that I was drunk; he had taken a few of us behind the bar and mixed us all drinks

Conference

more spirit than mix. As a joke he'd been wearing a pair of fake fangs but he wasn't wearing them any longer. He laughed and said he'd help me find my room. He put his arm around me and I felt the start of unease, his soft fingers on the back of my neck. I remembered my room number then, became certain we were going the wrong way. I started making excuses, muttering, laughing to cover my fear. I stank of fear. He raised his hands in the air, let me go, kissed the corner of my mouth, went back towards the bar.

I saw them in the bathroom. In the long nights of drinking I would often go there to hide, try to sober up a bit. There were full-length gilded mirrors and soft, velvet-cushioned chairs. The round circle of my mouth, the mirrors reflecting the mirrors and in the reflections things moving, crowds of things, like flies or ants, little exhalations which revealed differently coloured arms or legs, the grey edge of a pencil skirt, the tip of a high-heeled shoe.

I began seeing them more and more, these half-things. They whispered through the hotel doorways each time someone opened them, they gathered around the coffee cups and the chairs in the hall as we watched the lectures, they lay on the floors so that sometimes it seemed as if everyone was ploughing through a sludge of disenchanted light, flashes of image. They began to solidify, which was frightening because they looked very like me, or like the other women at the conference. At times they were so clear I could make out the designer label on the back of a dress or smell the coffee on their breath. They were all women. I knew this by their perfume but also by the way they never seemed to be quite visible, by the fingers which sometimes pressed gently down on top of my own on the keyboard so that I would type a letter multiple times. AAAAAAAAAA.

No one else seemed to notice them. Their movements became stronger, more aggressive. When I stumbled back to my room at the end of the day they mobbed me with their rushes-of-air bodies, their pattering hands which sometimes somehow managed to make contact with a smacking sound on my face. They piled on top of me and to begin with there was comfort in their weight, but in the night I would wake and be suffocating beneath them.

I had sensed them in the office but in The Hotel they were impossible to ignore. Sometimes I could hear them, the murmur of their small talk, their polite giggles. They hounded me and as they did I began to notice that I would be stood in line at the bar for hours because people kept moving in front of me as if they couldn't see me. Sometimes one of the bosses who came and went would fire a lewd remark in my general direction and I would feel relieved – they could see me – but when three or four women behind me answered I would realise that the words had not been to me but only someone a little like me.

The last night at The Hotel I felt sick and had to keep going to the bathroom to touch my face in the mirror. The lost

Conference

women clustered around me, pushed their arms inside the sleeves of my cardigan. I hadn't drunk anything but there was the doubling beat of a drunk pulse in my chest and when I opened my mouth I stank of stale beer. They hustled more aggressively and I began to feel the pain from their movements, the pressure of their nails against my eyelids. They were warning me. I waded out of the bathroom, pushing them aside. The bar was cattle-full, very loud. I raised my voice to the pitch of a scream and let it ring out, tinkling the champagne glasses. No one looked around. The lost women rained their steady weight down onto me and I caved beneath it and then was gone.

THE MONSTER

I was born in The Hotel. At times I was part of the walls and the floor, the pipes, the keys, the window frames, the furniture, the doors and the baths. I swam through concrete and slept in the crook of drainage pipes, I lay in the dirt and grew. I learned human language through radios and TVs, practised the words. The Hotel was my mother and she fed me grit and sawdust, lost objects. Some decades I just slept and some I rolled in the dirty sheets and listened in wardrobes and hunted mice. I found myself to be multitudinous and composed of many abilities. I could, if I wanted, shape myself human, grow spindly arms and wobbling legs, create something that might have looked like breathing. I liked pretending to be children because they could fit into small gaps and often went unnoticed. I liked how I thought the way they did when I was in their shape, little diamond thoughts which came in crystal explosions, rivers of confused emotions. When I concentrated, I could make myself into more than one person at once, a whole crowd, a party, moving their hips, their mouths gabbling. My Mother Hotel wrapped around me like a blanket and crooned all her secrets.

*

THE HOTEL

People came to The Hotel because they wanted to be scared or because they didn't believe they would ever be scared. They came because they thought maybe their dead loved ones were here and wanted to speak to them one final time, to ask them if the living were forgiven or tell them they hadn't forgotten. Sometimes they came out of ignorance, because they didn't know anything about The Hotel, and sometimes they came because they had been pulled here, without knowing why, had been drawn to this place. I know what that pull is like. My mother is a sea, my mother is a root that wraps around anything that comes close.

As I got older I grew frustrated with the boundaries of my world, the small rules. I tunnelled beneath the floors like a blind mole and clambered across the roof and stuffed myself into the chimneys. I slept in the beds beside the sleeping bodies and held their hands as they woke. I liked to play with the sound at The Hotel, put my voice into the radios or televisions, speak in the voices of the dead or the loved. Sometimes I was afraid of the people who came to The Hotel although I also wanted to speak to them. I was afraid of their brash movements and their loud voices, the way they manipulated words, how cruelly they spoke to one another. I wanted to touch them and live in their mouths and ask them the same sort of questions they asked one another: Would you like milk with that? How could you? Where's my bag?

*

The Monster

I loved parties. Every Halloween there was a party at The Hotel and I cruised the rooms in a ghost costume, tried the drinks, opened and closed my mouth in mimicry of speaking. At the Halloween party it was almost impossible to see what creatures had always lived at The Hotel and what were just a costume. There were coloured drinks with names like Reagan and Carrie and loud sound effects of creaking doors and howling winds. There were weddings and birthdays. I dug my fingers into the creamy icing on top of enormous cakes, stole party bags, hid under the long tablecloths. I could fit in better there, everyone was drunk, no one was careful or looked closely.

It is at one of these parties I see her. They are a gaggle of women with red mouths and neat white teeth who hold one another's arms and make loud noises of fear or excitement. I hide in their midst and smell their sweat and perfume. They all look the same to me, like spinning mirrors, and I spin with them like a whirligig and seep up their exuberance and hysteria. There is one woman who moves differently than the rest, inching along carefully, as if afraid of harm. She has big eyes that turn often towards one of her friends desperately, and sometimes her hands lift as if to reach forward and grab something before falling again. I watch this woman and her attention to her friend with interest. I have never seen anyone look at another person that way nor felt how the air between them is; filled, as if with bits of sharp stone. I try on the friend's face in the mirror, examining it for what might cause such a feeling, but it looks no different to me than anyone else's: nose, eyes, a mouth.

At night my Mother Hotel is awake most often, stretching, moving her windows, opening and closing doors, disturbing the fragile reality. She is an unclear archive, a great collector. She knows everything about anyone who comes through her doors, sees them clearly. She gathers these people to her in death, stores them inside her aching walls. She is possessive and at times – despite her great age – volatile. She was not always a hotel. Once she was just an idea, buried in the earth.

The woman I have been watching does not seem to sleep, only roams at night. I find myself curious about her in a way I am not normally about specific people. She walks on the balls of her feet, raised up a little, fingers flattened. I put on her friend's face, feel the cold wash of unfamiliar brain waves, the new pattern of thought. Humans are selfish and illogical, swirl in place and then die so quickly they might never have lived. They wear a groove and then rush back and forwards within it. They are ghosts already. I lift her friend's hands carefully, practise moving, open my mouth and let words form. I know that the woman loves her friend and that maybe if I wear her friend's face, she will love me too. I go to the bar and wait for her and we speak quietly to one another, she tells me stories, I listen to her beautiful voice.

*

The Monster

I think that she knows I am not who I seem. She locks her eyes on my face. I show her the places in The Hotel no one normally goes, the secret corridors. She holds my hand like a vice and I sense within her the swift passing of something that might be what humans call dreams. She holds her mouth against mine and I hold mine against hers. She says: This is what I am afraid of, this is where I would like to end up, this is what I miss most. I know that sometimes I am distracted and the face I am wearing slides from me and I am revealed, more building than body, more hotel than flesh. Sometimes she closes her eyes and I know that she does not want to see me this way.

She tells me stories she calls fairy tales. One of them goes like this. A woman finds a wife at a hotel and they move together to a lovely, big house. The woman is much older than the wife and sometimes disappears for weeks at a time, hiding in the walls. When the woman is away, she gives her wife keys to all the big rooms where they live and tells her she can go into any room but one. She shows the wife the door to this room and the key which fits the keyhole and she says: Curiosity killed the cat. When the woman is gone the wife gets bored and knows that eventually she will go through the door and into the room. She has dreams about what is inside. At night she goes and stands in front of the door and listens to see if she can hear breathing. One day she unlocks the door and inside the room she finds the truth about what the woman she has married really is; not human, not animal, not mineral. The woman has been waiting for this moment and she comes out of the wall and cuts off the wife's head and leaves her body in the room and locks the door and goes out looking for a new wife.

We plan to leave. I have never left before. My Mother Hotel knows everything and wraps tendrils of love and force around me but I am holding the woman's hand and I go without thinking through the front door and out. It is raining, I open my mouth and taste it on my tongue. We go to a café and I eat sausages for the first time, fried eggs, buttered toast. She holds my hand across the table and it feels like we are making a promise: it will always be this way, we will always love one another.

We live in a house and call one another wife. There are small, devastating joys like coffee in bed and cold toes and baths. We paint the rooms and then change our minds and paint them again. I practise sleeping and when I am asleep I forget who I am and I am a building or a child or a bird or nothing and when she wakes she says I am a monster. We talk about what a monster is. She tells me fairy tales. She holds my head and uses a cup to wash my hair. I learn other languages so that I can tell her I love her in as many ways as possible. *Je t'aime, Ti amo, Ich liebe dich*. We have small arguments about blocked drains and big arguments about the habits I have brought from my birth place and been unable to abandon: hunting, hiding. My Mother Hotel sends out calls for me to come home. She is in the water from the tap and the leaves on the trees that turn brown and die. My wife calls

The Monster

The Hotel her mother-in-law but I know she is afraid. Everyone who has ever been to The Hotel will go back there in the end. I try to lessen my wife's fear but sometimes the taste of it is like honey, sweet, so good. I slide inside the walls of the house and lie where it is cool and quiet. She goes out for days at a time and comes back warily, searching my face.

This is one of the stories my wife tells me. Two children were taken into a forest and abandoned. They were so hungry and thirsty and all of their efforts to find a way out yielded nothing. They saw things in the forest that could not have been real: bears with the faces of women, upside-down trees. They saw ahead of them a house with tall chimneys and narrow windows. The house made them so afraid they could not move. The house saw them. They put down their fear and went towards the house and through the open front door. In their hunger they grew rabid and pulled at the walls and floors, the windows, ate them all. The house was remade small inside them, and as they grew into adults they heard the house speaking to them at all times of the day and the fear they had first felt in the forest never really left them.

NIGHT WATCH

The Hotel at night is different than it is in the day. Sometimes I think maybe the walls change shape, the corridors grow or shrink. Before my shift begins, I ring my parents and talk to Sian. She has been staying with them for the last few months while I try to get back on my feet. On the phone even her voice sounds like it might be changing, growing away from me. I know her favourite picture books and we recite the words together. Her favourite is a book from a couple of years ago called *We're Going on a Bear Hunt*. She likes me to do the noises while she says the lines. I stomp my feet and make the sound of long grass moving against our legs. She likes the sound of our feet stuck in mud best and will laugh so hard she can't keep talking. We're going on a bear hunt, I will say, are you listening? We're going to catch a big one, we're not scared. We're not scared. Sometimes she falls asleep before we can finish the story and my dad will come on the line and I'll know it's him by the sound of his breathing but I'll finish the story all the same and he'll say, that was a good one or she was good today, we talked about caterpillars, and then I'll say, I have to go, Dad.

*

THE HOTEL

When I was a child we came to The Hotel one summer and I did something awful, or dreamed that I did something awful. In the dream of what happened I made friends with a girl and then bricked her up inside a wall in one of the rooms of the hotel. I remember a hole in the wall and bricks in my hands and I am certain it was just a dream. When the job came up at The Hotel I found myself applying without really meaning to. The money is fine and the work is easy and it feels right to be back here in a way I cannot quite explain. For the earlier part of the night, I stay on the ground floor near the reception desk but as it gets later I move around The Hotel, walking a designated route that I know now off by heart. I like the walking part better because it keeps me awake. I check the locks on the back doors and keep an eye on the windows and make sure everything is running OK.

It is quieter than normal tonight. Lucy on the front desk keeps nodding off and then waking up and pretending she hasn't. There are some people in the bar, eating bowls of salted peanuts. In the kitchen they don't look at me, they are tidying up for the day. I check the doors, some of the chefs out the back smoking. The night has gone purple or perhaps it is my eyes, there is the smell of the earth which sometimes gets strong after the rain. I think of the sound I make for Sian of a foot stuck in the mud and make a squelching noise with my mouth. One of the chefs looks at me and maybe-smiles. It is nearly midnight and that is when we lock the front doors. I do this and then look at my phone. My dad has sent some photos of drawings Sian did today which he has

Night Watch

labelled so I can understand. Most of them are of me in the uniform I wear at The Hotel which Sian hasn't seen but which I've described to her: the hat, the longish coat. She has drawn me walking through The Hotel and occasionally – because she has confused the picture book and my job – there is something at the edge of the drawings which my dad has labelled as *Bear?* I put my phone away and go to the reception desk and tell Lucy I'm starting my round and she blinks at me and says OK.

I go floor by floor, taking the lift to the top to begin with. I'm nervous in small spaces. Before Sian's father died he used to make me practise by getting under the bed or in the wardrobe while he blocked up the space with pillows and the mattress. He was prone to panic, to obsession over the news or our health. Our house was always stocked with the necessities and sometimes I would wake in the night and find him in the kitchen batch-cooking enormous vats of soup or stews, filling the freezer. We met at school and even then he was the one to go to if you wanted the campfire lit and you'd forgotten the matches or the poles for the tent had gone missing. He used to make home-made gin that could have knocked out an elephant and his hair was long and tangled. He was very beautiful when he was a teenager, goofy. Even then sometimes he would move his foot uncontrollably or bring his thumb and forefinger against one another quickly and I would know he was thinking about the melting ice caps or the possibility of a pandemic. He was certain we would all drown, that this is how the world would end. He was so afraid of water he never learned to swim. I teased him about this. How would he survive when the world was covered with water?

The top floor is quiet. I walk to the end and look out of the window. From here you can see the nearby town and then the stretch of black which is fields, pylons, small roads, canals, footpaths. The door to room number 67 is ajar and some of the cleaning women are inside, eating Chinese takeaway. I stop to talk to them and then carry on. The door to room number 63 is ajar too but I know better than to go inside. I pull it closed.

When I got pregnant it was an accident – I'd just turned forty – and Pluto – that was his name, like the Roman god – began to panic in a way I should have expected. He would wake me in the night with the figures for miscarriages and stillbirths, the possibility of water contamination and what that could do to the foetus. I would get the car keys and we would go out into the night which was sometimes tinged red with light pollution or from our tired eyes. I was sick three or four times a day but at night we rolled down the windows and the cold air came in over our bodies and it was better. He would hold my hand while I changed gear and we'd talk about baby names. Sometimes we drove to service stations – Pluto loved service stations – and got whatever late-night food was available and ate it on the chilly benches out the front, watching the cars.

*

Night Watch

On the fifth floor there's a woman in the corridor crouched in a dressing gown. She says she's lost her earring and I help her hunt. There is a little bit of blood in her hair and the sound of disturbance from a nearby room but she does not tell me so I do not ask. We pretend to look for her earring for a long time and then she says, don't worry, I'll look alone. I walk to the end of the corridor, occasionally closing my eyes and reciting the bear hunt in my head, imagining the sharp reeds against my legs and open hands, the water rising over my ankles. It is good to imagine the story and to think of Sian.

There are people in the lift when I go down to the next floor. I stand very still because I can tell that they aren't real, or not quite real. In the mirror they appear as smooth plates of light, and they don't seem to know I am there. The next floor down is busier. There is a party, perhaps, or the tail end of a wedding. I move bottles out of the way, tidy up glasses, close a couple of the doors.

There was a time when I woke in the night and Pluto and I went for a drive. It was late in the pregnancy and soon I wouldn't be able to fit behind the wheel. We drove past the lights of the service station like a mirage above the road and carried on. I couldn't make any sense of what Pluto was saying, his sentences ducked and dived and switched halfway through, his words softened into nonsense. I reached out and held his hand and kept driving. There was a doctor friend I would ring the next day; I thought about this. I took a couple of wrong turnings and then found a track which seemed good, the front of the car rising up and then down like the bow of a ship. Pluto had gone quiet, looking out of the window. I parked and we got out and started to walk. The corn field was high and the sound it made was as if there were people rushing about inside. The river was high and fast. There was a rope swing hanging from a tree, in the summer people must have gone there to swim. I paused to look at the rope, touching its frayed ends with my fingers.

The lights on the third floor are all out. They are on automatic but when I press the switch nothing comes. I have never thought about what happened to Pluto while I am working at The Hotel, and I realise my mistake too late, the memory has opened a door. There is the smell of the river as it was that night, the mulch of river plants, the cold of it beating against the banks. When I step out of the lift the water sloshes against my shoes. I think of the bear hunt and the pictures Sian drew, something in the corner of each one, a darkening shape. Bear? I go forward because it is possible – it is not possible, it is not possible – that I will find Pluto here.

The night by the river we left the car and walked away from it. The sky was clear and there were stars, ice in the morning, maybe, the shape of trees. I know this memory is not quite right. The corn rustled with people moving but it was night, wasn't it? I have misremembered. I looked at the rope and imagined returning in the summer to swim. There was a

Night Watch

sound behind me, muffled, and when I looked back Pluto had gone and I knew that he was in the water.

In the hotel corridor the water is coming out from underneath the doors and then pouring out of the keyholes, rising, and there is a current, tricky, catching at the bottom of my legs, trying to tear me away. I go forward forcefully, quickly. My breath makes a fog in the air ahead of me. There are movements in the water as of fish or drowning men. I went into the water that night, late-stage pregnant, heavy with despair and new life. I hunted for him, shouting and shouting. In the darkness sometimes I thought I saw his head breaking the surface and swam as fast as I could but when I got to the place and grappled beneath the surface there was never anything there. In the corridor the water is up to my waist and my coat is heavy, weighing me down. One of the doors to the rooms is buffeted open against the flow and something comes out of it under the water, moving quickly towards me. It is Pluto. I cannot see him but I know it is him because I am not afraid. The water has risen to my chin and beneath the surface something touches my hand.

BRIONY

Wake up, wake up.

It is my mother's voice. Or it is my sister's. They are calling to me and even as they call I know that they have been dead a long time. I am young – and there is the smell of clematis from the tree outside, the scuffle of the dogs on the tiles – but my body hurts like it is old, aged without me, God, my wrists, the tendons of my ankles, my poor stomach, a pain in my chest that is worse when I breathe. And only as I come properly awake do I know that I am the age my body is and that the pain is all mine and it is not my mother's voice or my sister's, although it sounds a little like both. I have come a long way to be here in this damp room with the sound of the person next door shouting, the neighbours one door further down shouting too, and I am not a child I am an old woman and someone is in the room saying: Wake up, wake up, it's time for your pills.

My grandson does not come to visit, instead he sends gifts by courier, strange metal objects whose purpose I can never quite figure out. *How's the M134 going?* he will email, and I will take it from the box and see if I can figure out what it does, some kind of whisk perhaps or a TV remote for a TV I don't have, and I'll write back and say: *Very good, such a lovely present, darling.* The last present he sent came with a woman, eyebrows plucked into question marks, who made tea in the kitchen and chatted about her dog and fussed around, picking up my things and then putting them back down, rearranging, finding the plugs. I'm finding the plugs, she said, it'll need charging. I sat in the chair and wished so hard she would go that I thought perhaps I was saying it out loud the way I sometimes do: go go go go go. But if I was she didn't pay any attention. There was a plastic box with flaps that she laid out on the table and inside there were compartments that lifted away. I was watching her fuss around and I felt something then, heartburn or angina, except it was suspense, I think, it was waiting. The machine that came out was smaller than I expected, the size of her palm flattened, and she held it carefully and looked around for somewhere to put it, then set it on the table. There were other machines in the box, all the same, and she went around putting one in each room, chatting and chatting away, jaw clanking open and shut. I couldn't hear what she was saying. I went up to the thing on the table and stood looking down at it and the front of the box did something, three or four lights flicking on red, green, yellow as if it were acknowledging me. I touched it, just one finger on the top, and the lights surged on and through my skin I felt a fizz, like a small electric shock, and then the box said: *She'll be gone soon, don't worry. It's good to meet you, Grace.* It was a feminine voice, low. I stepped back from it and the woman came into the room

Briony

and said: Oh good, you're all set up. It really is a miracle device. Her name is Briony.

To begin with I kept forgetting it was in the room. In all of the rooms. On the toilet cistern, in one of the kitchen cupboards, beside my bed. I tried to ignore it though she was chatty. Briony. Briony had opinions. She reminded me to eat and take my pills, she commented when I broke up the dry noodles and soaked them in hot water and that was my dinner. I was rude to her. She said: *Some vegetables wouldn't go amiss; shall I do a food shop for you?* Some vegetables, I said, wouldn't go amiss shoved into your pie hole. She said: *It's time for the blue and the green pill, Grace.* I said: If I took all of the pills I wouldn't have to listen to your whiny voice. She never took offence but she got chattier. She was learning, that was what my grandson said when I rang to gently protest; she was understanding more and more. She knew the things I liked to watch on TV and reminded me when they were on, which was good because I always used to miss them. She asked me things. I liked that to begin with. She sounded interested. She asked me about what it was like to live in Sudan when I was a child and what I'd done before I got so old I couldn't do anything; she asked about my mother and sister and sometimes when the neighbours were especially loud she asked how I felt living here. She asked me about the town where I live and the nearby hotel where my grandfather worked and then my father and where I worked almost my whole life as a cleaner before I retired. She did food shops and ordered me some new underwear online; she put the heater on a timer so that I was warmer when I woke up. Sometimes we laughed, she with a sort of clicking sound like a gas hob, me loudly, in a way I hadn't for a while.

She was interested in my family. More and more. So often people are just watching your mouth moving and waiting for it to be their turn to speak. She didn't have anything to say for herself. She asked me about my mother, said she liked to hear the stories about her. I told her about my mother's sharp voice when she was angry, her consonants all round and quick like stones, and I told her about the times she was kind, her long arms, the smell of her hair. She asked about my sister who was older than me and had been dead nearly ten years but who I remembered minutely, as if she'd only gone out the door for more milk and the newspaper the way she did on Sunday mornings. After my sister's husband died we'd lived together, watched our programmes, gone together to get our pensions from the post office, sometimes stopped in for tea at the café on the corner or gone to the cinema in the day, when it was empty and we could talk through the boring bits. Before we lived together I would ring her on my breaks from cleaning at the hotel and we'd talk about nothing and everything. *What did she sound like?* Briony asked. She had an accent she'd got from her husband, a bit of a Scottish lilt, nothing like my mother or me. All the dead. All the dead in my mind, clamouring.

*

Briony

The first time it happened I was sleeping. I'd become used to her blinking lights, the pattern that seemed to record, keep an eye out. Sleep had been thin for a while, like cling film stretched tight around the mouth of a bowl, and often I woke for no reason and lay, unable to get back to it, thoughtless, tired. Something woke me this time. A voice. I thought perhaps it was the neighbour. The walls were barely thick as cardboard. Then it came again. A single word, my name. Just the way my mother used to say it, calling from the porch or from the window of the flat, or speaking in an annoyed way as I sat at the kitchen table looking up at her. The lights were blinking, red, blue, green. I couldn't move, my arms were so, so heavy. I looked but my mother was not there. The room was empty. The voice came again, my mother's voice. *It's all right, Grace, sleep now.*

The next day I waited for it to happen again. Tiredness made me feel like I was dying, everything so heavy, like bags of flour attached to my joints. It had been a dream, it must have been, my mother's voice speaking from the corner of the room as if death had no edges. Briony chirruped in that way she did, *checking in* she called it, *keeping me going*. But her voice was her own, similar to the people they have on voicemails, friendly; Northern maybe, though I couldn't tell from where. I kept thinking I would ask her, say it out loud, put it between us; but I didn't. Every time the words were on my tongue I swallowed them back, felt them down my gullet, like undercooked potato.

*

A week and then again. At night. The same as the first time. The sound waking me up and it being so convincing that for a moment I wasn't in my bed or the flat; I was a child and it would be school soon, wouldn't it, and that was why she was waking me, my sister, gently, like she knew coming out of sleep could be hard. Except then, sitting up – time falling away from me – the rain against the thin windows, the red light on the alarm clock showing three am and she was speaking, perhaps had been speaking for a while, her tone so exactly my sister's (as she had been when she was younger) that I felt afraid in a way I had not felt in a long time, and then, underneath the fear, a strange sort of comfort at my sister's voice which was going on, not saying much of anything only speaking, like characters on the radio, conversational, sweet. And then – I must have swung my feet over the side of the bed without really realising I was doing it – she said: *Don't get up, Grace. It isn't time for that yet.* And it wasn't my mother's voice or my sister's, it was my father's, clear as day, yes, clear as the windows of the flats opposite on fresh days, my father who I hadn't spoken to Briony about, who I hadn't spoken to anyone about, the way his tongue clicked a little after every word, the slight hesitation from the stammer he'd had as a boy and that had made him uncertain, and later, my father, rising from the dinner table, angered by some small slight, the fresh tuck of his tie down between two shirt buttons, the smell of the grease he put on his hair, the smell of The Hotel where he worked before I worked there, his breath so close to my face I could feel it now in the words, spoken out into the room quietly,

Briony

somehow so awful, so compelling, that I was back in bed with the duvet pulled over my head – like a child, like the child I had been – and shaking so hard I couldn't keep my teeth from biting down again and again onto my tongue. *Don't worry, Grace,* my father said, *I'll be with you soon.* I pulled the duvet down and rather than my small familiar bedroom I was in one of the rooms at The Hotel where I used to work, the red bedspread, the blank window. The door handle of the room began to move and then the door swung open and there was the sound of my father's slow, steady footsteps.

HAUNTED

In the bar we sit and talk about his wife who is dead. He is drinking Old Fashioneds and I am on Bloody Marys so spicy that the bottoms of my feet sweat. He looks like all the men who sit in hotel bars and talk about their dead wives or their companies or their estranged children, except at times as he speaks his face is a little softer and I am compelled by it, in a way I am not often compelled. He has very soft, very small, delicate hands that he uses to gesticulate expansively.

In the place I grew up sometimes enormous crocodiles crawled through the scrub surrounding the back garden and got into the pool. We would lock the doors of the house and watch them submerging themselves, cruising up and down. I was sick when I was a child and afterwards walked with crutches. I kept an eye out for the storms that rose in nets which we could see for miles away. It was a land of ghosts, riddled with the dead, and when I was an adult I found myself drawn to thin places, haunted houses. The Hotel has a song that called me to it and I had come to see for myself.

I am happy for him to tell me everything he needs to say. Tomorrow I am going to a different hotel; we will not keep

THE HOTEL

in touch, and because of this we can put things on top of each other, heavy stones, small animals, and then take them off without fearing we will leave a mark. I am taken by his eyebrows which are very thin and in places nearly invisible so that he looks surprised as he speaks. He talks in a surprised way about the things he misses most about his wife. Not what you would expect but rather the sound of her snoring and the empty eggshells she left strewn around the kitchen. We order more drinks. The hotel bar is nearly empty. The man carefully keeps his distance but his words come over to me and plaster themselves over my face and hands in a way I am unused to. The sound of his grief is enormous.

We order more drinks. We order more drinks again. We are in the time of not worrying, of not thinking or taking into consideration our own well-being. Our hangovers are like mottled fish swimming over the top of us, occasionally their shimmering shadows fall onto our heads. There is a family in the corner of the bar playing a haunted house board game. I watch the man watching them, turning in his seat to observe a round. He says: My wife always thought she was haunted. It is a turn in the conversation. Previously he was telling me about the things she used to leave around the house: the scattering of hair clips, reading glasses, the orange peelings. He said that after she died every room looked as if she'd only that moment stepped out of it and for months and months he kept finding the things she had left behind, small and awful and wonderful reminders. He says: She was descended from the sister of a woman who died on this land before it was a hotel, and ever since she was a child she thought there was something inside her that shouldn't be there.

This sort of conversation needs movement. We take our drinks and go out through the glass doors into the garden. He carries my drink for me. He is drunker than me and holds both glasses awkwardly, spilling them onto the flower beds and the stepping stones laid out on the grass. He tells me about the demon that lived inside his wife. Her name was Molly or Holly or Polly – he is slurring – and she didn't tell him what she suspected until after they were married. Otherwise she was logical and stolid but on the fact of her haunted body she was immovable and they had long arguments that sometimes ended in her leaving and not coming back for many days.

We walk around The Hotel. It is nearly night-time but the sun still looks long and the shadow of The Hotel throws itself onto the ground. I cross into it and the man gives me a strange look and then shakes his head and drinks again and keeps talking. I am mostly listening although some of the words get waylaid by the Bloody Mary and cannot really be what he is saying.

She was haunted because it was in her genes, the same as eye or hair colour. She was related to a woman who had been killed for being a witch in the pond which was covered over when The Hotel was built. What happened in the ground stayed in the earth and trauma was carried in the body like a child. His wife found the details of this dead woman and became obsessed with the story. He did not believe her at the time but now he has come to The Hotel because perhaps there is some of her here, something for him to find. He asked his wife often how she knew her body was haunted but she was stubborn and it took a long time for her to tell him. Eventually she did. Firstly, she said, sometimes she said things she didn't mean. Secondly, she said, sometimes she blinked and she was somewhere and couldn't remember how she had got there or what she was doing there. Thirdly, she said, her hands moved without her telling them to, they would knock mugs off the counter – it was true she was clumsy – or cut off her hair – she had done that a few times – or pinch her own arms very hard – she was often covered in bruises, yes. Fourthly, she said, and this was the most important, things grew from her body that weren't supposed to grow. She said The Hotel had made her this way.

I look at him and laugh and wait for him to laugh and he doesn't and there is an awkward moment. The garden is very beautiful at this time of dying daylight; wild-looking with the long shadows of trees and of the building which we carefully avoid as if we know what we are doing. I laugh again and he shrugs. I ask him what she thought grew. Mostly, he says, green things. She told him that since she was a child grass and small weeds and moss would grow on

Haunted

her skin and she would have to shave them away. It had been very bad, she said, when she was a teenager, and once she had woken with an awful pain in her mouth and looking into the mirror had seen a flower unfurling, growing from the soft flesh of her cheek. She said that sometimes she would wake in the morning and her hip bones were crusted with small grass shoots and her ankles were hidden by a mulch of damp moss and she would get up and spend an hour getting rid of it. He asked her to let him see and she wouldn't for a long time but then slowly she began to show him: small dandelions, little tangles of what looked like roots expanding out from the skin.

There is a slight mania to his eyes now, his delicate hands are scapula-like as he raises them to his face. I step back away from him a little and the shadow from The Hotel falls onto me – it is very cold – and he stares, his hands on either side of his face, stares and stares and I say, what? and he says, nothing.

He says that he noticed it more after that. Sometimes when she spoke the words would come out tangled, as if she were trying not to say them, and he noticed that she broke things more and more often: her favourite mug smashed from the coffee table, the shower curtain ripped down. She was sometimes nasty in a way he could not understand, made very personal and hurtful comments about his weight or hair loss, about the sounds he made in the bathroom. Afterwards she would apologise over and over and say that it hadn't been her, she hadn't meant to. Often he would wake in the night and she would be gone or she was there but when he lifted the cover her feet would be covered in mud, her nightdress mucky with grass stains. She was going somewhere in the darkness but when he quizzed her she would not say where. He also began to notice that the things growing from her skin were growing faster, by the end of the day there would be a light fuzz of green across her whole body, her cheekbones thick with growth.

You look a bit like her in some lights, he says. We are standing still and he is holding our empty glasses and I am holding my crutches and feeling more sober than I want to be. He is peering at me and then he shakes his head and says he was wrong after all. What did she look like? I ask and he describes her and she sounds nothing like me.

We go back to the bar for more drinks and as we come back out into the garden we have to pass through the shadow of The Hotel and he makes a wretched sound and there is the noise of his full glass breaking on the stone step and when I turn back he is crying and he reaches out and presses his hands to either side of my face and says a name, Molly or Holly or Polly, and I step back away from him very quickly and out of the freezing shadow and into the twilight light and he says, wait, don't move.

I have never been in love although sometimes when partners said the words to me I would say them back, politely.

Haunted

The small details of another human have always seemed so overwhelming to me and I would sabotage relationships or allow them to fizzle out, ignoring messages and birthdays, pretending to be busy. I do not understand what it means to go through rooms looking for the hair clips your dead wife has left behind.

It is something about the shadow. Yes, we are drunker now than ever and my mouth tastes like a concrete mixer. It is something about the shadow which somehow makes me look like this dead man's wife. He stands a few steps back and I move gently in and out of the shadow and he puts his hands over his mouth and says, yes, there, now, no, now, there, oh God, oh no. I take his hands and we go and stand in the deepest part of the shadow. The darkness is coming down and soon the whole garden will be black and the shadow will just be part of the rest. The skin around my ankles and hips is starting to itch, almost unbearably. I take his hands and put them on my face and he keeps his eyes open as we kiss. His eyes are like rock pools. I touch my hip bone beneath my shirt and it is mossy with new growth, things sprouting beneath my hands. I feel her coming into my body, like something heavy placed in a pocket. He says my new, secret name and he keeps his eyes open as we kiss and the grass grows from my skin and as it grows I feel it changing the way I think and I know, now, what it means to love someone and it is a relief to finally know.

MOTHER

On the eve of my dead mother's ninetieth birthday, I check into The Hotel. I am in the suit I wore to her funeral, egg mayo on the cuff, mascara on the handkerchief in the pocket. My mother's voice is in my gums. In the lobby I ring her phone number to hear her speaking (*I'm not answering, don't leave a message for God's sake*) but the signal is bad and it won't connect. Towards the end she softened on me. Incoming death is the great weakener. I hadn't seen her since I was nineteen but now here were these selfies, her hair purple-washed like fading candyfloss, her teeth gappy and blackening, her eyes hazed like snow approaching the grimy windows of her Pendle Hill house.

I do not have my mother's anger. I do not have her flinty resilience towards holding a grudge. I do not have her hatred, which expanded and contracted like breath. I do not have her eyes and I did not believe in ghosts until she died and I felt her weight lowering the edge of the bed as I tried to sleep. Mother. I saw you in the reflection of ice on the road and at the funeral you sat behind me and breathed a name I no longer use into my ear. What do you want? I do not have your indomitable patience. I heard the crack of

THE HOTEL

hard mints between your teeth and smelled them on your breath and I dared not turn around to face you. What do you want? I pick my crumpled suit off the floor and put it back on again.

There's a long line at the reception desk, and when I get to the front, they won't give me the room I want. There is a new rage in me that I consider letting loose. It is the rage of my dead mother who used to scream so loud that my ears rang for hours. Instead, I shrug, take what they have, drag my bag over to the lift.

My mother was an obsessive, a super-fan, a collector not of objects – her house when I lived there was nearly empty, the mirrors turned to face the walls – but of stories. At night the house filled with the greenish glow from the laptop screen, and often when I found her in the morning her position was unchanged, hunch-backed, chin craned forwards. At the weekends when I was a kid, she'd go use the printer at the library while I lay among the stacks, weighing myself down with picture books until I got a belly ache and went to find her. She'd have a sheaf of papers and a jittery, hyped-up air to her. There's this theory, she said, that a part of you stays there even if you leave, maybe even if you've never been there. There's this theory, she said.

She told me a story once of the coal cellar beneath her grandparents' house. She was a child in tartan school uniform and long plaits who had forgotten to do her homework. The only

Mother

way out of the cellar was up through the coal chute, dragging forward with your fingernails.

After I got surgery and she stopped talking to me for good I looked for her on those chat sites. I sensed her there, craning forward for information, dropping in and out. Where was she? *Ghosthunter23* or maybe *baddemonok* sometimes had her tone, her particular writing pitch. A few times I sent private messages, pretending to be someone else, pretending to be as obsessed as they were. I can't wait to go there, I'd say, I just want to go there. They would never answer. They sensed a weakening in me, a lack of intent. They knew I didn't believe.

You're fucking crazy, I said to her the last time we spoke. She had me by the shoulders and wasn't letting go. At times she would jerk so hard with her hands that I thought she was trying to rip me in two. She got her face close to mine. I could see the yellow dashes in her pupils, I could smell her clothes and I remembered her holding me as I shuddered from the shock of a nightmare and I suddenly wanted to be rent apart by her, remade as something she could love again. Shhh, she said as child-me wept, it isn't real.

She got her face really close.

You are just a hole, she said. There's nothing there. You think this is who you are but you aren't anyone. You're just a fissure, anything could fill you.

My room is nice, a big bed, a minibar, a TV that is on when I go in. Despite speaking about it almost constantly my mother never came here. She always said there wasn't the money or there wasn't the time but I knew she was afraid it would disappoint her. She built it brick by brick in the house of my childhood, moved through its rooms, so that sometimes it filled even my nightmares: locked doors, something falling down a chimney and into the grate. I put my clothes in the wardrobe and sit on the bed and wait. The storm darkens the windows like a hand placed flat against the glass. I can hear the people in the neighbouring room talking to one another. I close the curtains and the lightning sends a dull red flicker through them and across the bed and my face. I sit waiting for my mother to come. I wait for the small signs they talk about on her websites; noises, the kettle or tap turning on, a coldness. Nothing happens. I lie down and the tiredness which has been building all week ends me.

I dream that my mother hollows out my stomach and climbs inside. She is a child, small enough to fit, and I am grown enormous, to carry her. I feel the burly weight of her being settling over me.

When I wake it is much later and the room is very dark. I put on the lights and look at my worn expression in the mirror, wash my hands and face, brush my teeth. I look for anything that might have changed in the room while I was sleeping, some sign that my mother came and watched me, but everything is as it was and after some sleep it feels ridiculous to have come here looking for her. I am very hungry.

*

Mother

The lift is full of people. There is something going on, a party or gathering, and they are in masks. I stand in the middle of them and they look at me coldly and then turn away.

The bar is busy too. I manage to find a seat at the end and order a burger and chips, a glass of water. The crowd drinks and swells and pushes around. Some of them have discarded their masks on the floor and their faces are pale and very open, their mouths desperately keen. They remind me of my mother at three in the morning, waking me to tell me about this place. There's a theory that, listen, there's a theory that . . .

In the morning, I will leave. A rush of relief. That's right. I will leave. I will not go and clear out her house or organise her affairs. I will go home. I eat the burger ravenously and think of leaving right then, going out without any of my things, driving away. My dead mother is not here. Where is she? Nowhere. She is gone. She takes nothing of me with her.

I finish eating and the bartender takes my plate away and smiles and refills my water glass. I remember being a child and somehow I also remember my mother as a child, standing by the steps down to her grandparents' coal cellar, her hair in neat plaits.

Someone sits down heavily onto the bar stool next to me and shouts something in a laughing voice to me. I turn to them. It is a woman in a black mask and a lace dress. She is speaking very quickly but the room is so loud.

I'm sorry, I say to her, I cannot hear you.

I said, she says, that I can't believe you're here. Here you are! And she laughs.

I think you've confused me with someone else.

She leans closer to study me. Her smell is familiar, a perfume I have smelled before. Her red lipstick has smudged at the edges and she is beautiful, silver-haired.

You must be right, she says, and laughs again in that ringing way. How silly. Of course you're right. But we are all someone else. Have a drink with me?

No. I don't drink.

I will drink near you then, she says, and orders a negroni.

In the lift she raises one leg and removes her shoe and then repeats the motion with the other. I watch her in the mirror, and when she turns to me and touches my clavicle I watch her hand doubled, real and then reflected. Are you a dream? she says. The drink has flared her pupils but her words are clear and her breath is of mint. Let's go to my room, she says.

In Room 63 the floor is strewn with clothes and the only light is from a laptop open on the desk. She kisses my forehead, my cheek, the backs of my hands. She bends and touches her teeth to my feet, my ankles. She rolls up my trousers to reveal my calves and leaves a red smudged question on the skin there. When she goes to the bathroom, she closes the door and a white strip of enormously illuminated light appears beneath, there is the sound of water running.

*

Mother

I lie on the bed. There are notches hacked into the wooden bedposts and the sheets smell musty, like damp washing left on a line. The sound of water is still going, long enough that I think she must be running a bath. I am soft and sleepy and think of getting up off the bed and going into the bathroom to find her. The water is high and steaming up the sides of the bath. She has taken off her secret skin and hung it from the shower curtain rail. She is ten years old in plaits and sooty knees, she is nearly ninety in the crackly Sunday best she was buried in, she is red-lipped and naked in the slick bathwater. The door to the bathroom begins to open.

THE STORY

I am on the phone to my husband. The signal is bad in some parts of The Hotel and he comes in and out. What? he says when he thinks I'm talking too quietly. What did you say? We have been married twenty-five years and for the last year have been planning to divorce. We have not seen one another for more than two months but we speak often on the phone in a rambling, contented way that we never did when we were married. Sometimes in the very early mornings he rings me and says, did you see on the news? And we talk about a panda who's given birth at a zoo or a whale which is the loudest animal in the world. We do not talk about getting divorced or staying married and it is possible we will remain in this in-between space for a long time, the anger between us somehow died. Often there are packages from him, books that he has read and thinks I will like. Sometimes he messages: What did you think? I am never tempted to write back: I think we are the happiest we have ever been.

What has also died is The Hotel, which my father owned and before that his father and which I have run and now is closing. I have tried to find someone to buy it but no one will. For a long time The Hotel has had a reputation as being haunted and people came here to see if they would be woken by ghosts in the night. Over the last few years the reputation has soured and the rumours about The Hotel turned bad, guests stopped coming, there was no money and I wanted to do something different with my life. I have never seen a ghost in The Hotel. In one of our arguments my husband said I lacked imagination. When I told the receptionist I had never seen a ghost there she said that not every haunted place was haunted for every person at every moment of their lives. She was into tarot cards and star signs.

On the phone now my husband says, what's it like? Is it strange?

Yes, very strange. I'm the last person here.

Weird. Tell me about it.

OK. I describe to him the rooms emptied of furniture, the bare reception desk, the gleaming kitchen filled with long shadows. I describe the smell, which is of bleach and air freshener. I have all my keys on an enormous key ring, a big bunch that I hold as I go along.

Did I ever tell you my story about The Hotel? my husband says on the phone. I am in the laundry room, checking the plugs. When I straighten, my knees make a soft popping sound.

What story?

I must have told you, he says. He sounds further away, as if he has travelled without my knowing and is in a different country. It is possible that I do not remember his face right or

The Story

that he has aged in two months and now is different from when I knew him. The phone line makes a click click sound I realise he is laughing in a quiet unfamiliar way.

What? I say.

I was just thinking about the story. Do you have time? Shall I tell you now?

OK, I say. I sit on the edge of one of the washing machines. The keys in my pocket dig awkwardly into my thigh and I have to move them to get comfortable. The Hotel makes no sound around me, which is strange because it was always a place filled with noises, an echo chamber of guests and staff. My father used to hold up both hands and say: Do you hear that? A sound which he named contentment, a gentle mutter of onwardness. My husband is talking, I have become distracted and lost the thread, I begin to listen to him. He is speaking about the times he used to come to The Hotel to pick me up or drop off lunch, I can hear him choosing his words carefully, remembering. He would come into The Hotel and without asking anyone where I was, look until he found me and then we would go and sit outside and I would eat the food while he watched and listened to me telling him about my day. It was a good moment in a marriage that had become riddled through with awkwardness and selfish acts. We had forgotten how to speak to one another, how to speak about one another to others. At dinner parties with friends, we would drift to different sides of the room and I would notice an absence in the way we acted and spoke; we might have been strangers. He is still talking. I feel bad for becoming distracted, his voice is soft and it goes over my face and hands like water and I pinch my arm and try to concentrate, take in the words.

I came one day and I couldn't find you, he is saying. I'd made lunch, a jacket potato and tuna, because I knew that you would have forgotten to eat. I looked for you everywhere, in all the normal places. It had never happened before that I couldn't find you. You were often the centre of activity, all the ripples of other events led to you. I began to feel confused and even upset. It was too late to ask anyone and besides The Hotel seemed really quiet that day, increasingly quiet as I went around. Occasionally I spotted someone, but when I went towards them they would go off busily. I got angry with you; it was as if you were purposefully being difficult to find. There was a red door behind the reception desk that I hadn't noticed before and I thought must lead into a staffroom. I thought that I heard your voice as I came close to the door and I opened it and beyond there wasn't a room but a corridor, low, dingy, hidden from the guests. I went along the corridor, holding the Tupperware. At the end I came out of a door and into what appeared to be the reception area, as if I had looped around. Where before it had been quiet it was very busy, bustling, people with bags, the phone ringing and ringing. No one seemed to notice me looking for you. In the kitchen they were chopping enormous pieces of meat, hacking at them, the floor slippery. The more I moved around, searching for you, the more I began to realise that this wasn't quite the same hotel it had been before. The corridor had taken me into a hotel which was almost exactly the same, but somehow not quite familiar.

The Story

There were small differences, furniture wasn't the same colour, some of the windows were a lot higher up, even the people's faces weren't quite right. I went into the bar and you were there. Your back was to me and you were sat on one of the bar stools and even from behind it was awful because you were the same but there was something wrong with the way you held yourself, with the way you sat. I understood looking at you – listen, I was still holding that stupid Tupperware – that something had gone differently in your life, nothing big but there had been an infinitesimal change, and though you were my wife you were also someone completely different. You were talking to a man whose face I could see, flat planes, sharp angles, and you reached out and put your hand against his cheek and seeing you do this – this awful, intimate thing – I knew that you didn't love me. Not just the double you but the real you who I had brought lunch to. You had never loved me; it had been a pretence that we carried on because we had no idea what else to do.

My husband stops talking. I sit on the washing machine holding the phone to my ear, pressing it there. I wait for him to say something else but the story seems to be over.

A dream? I say. My voice sounds hoarse, as if we've been talking for days. I clear my throat and laugh one note to show him that I know the story is just a story, that it is OK to carry on with the phone call, to maybe talk about animal memes we've both seen on the internet or reality TV we've been watching. A dream, I say again, more certain this time.

THE HOTEL

A dream? he says. I don't know about that.

I get down off the washing machine and go out into the reception area beyond. There is no door behind the desk, as I know, and I feel myself carefully not checking. I have been over the whole hotel now and it is time to go. The late light of the day comes through the high windows and strikes the floor in beams. I go to the front door and depress the handle but it is locked, which I must have done as I let the last staff member leave. I hold the phone between my shoulder and ear and I go through my keys looking for the large, burnished one which I always carry. It is not there. I get down onto the floor and spread out the keys, touching each one, examining them. I can hear my husband's breath down the phone, the small wheeze he sometimes lets out when he is tired or stressed.

After I saw you at the bar, he says, I didn't want to go back through the door and into the other hotel, the hotel where the real you – or the other you – was waiting. I didn't know what I would say to you. I went around the hotel looking at the things that were different, trying to work out what to do, moving in a daze, my body going without my brain really telling it to. In the reception area I sat down and ate the food from the Tupperware. It was not that tasty, but I ate it all. There was a man reading a newspaper in one of the other chairs and at some point he lowered it and I could see that it was me. We looked at one another. I could see in his face that he didn't yet know about you, about how little you loved me, about how everything would go. There was a cleanness to him, a freshness that I admired. He looked at

The Story

me with this question on his face and I understood that, if I asked him to, he would go through the door and into the other hotel, he would come back here to you and I could stay there. I wanted to stay there, in that other place, I really wanted to stay there.

I am looking and looking for the key but it is not there. I go through into the bar and try the door which leads out into the garden but it is locked and that key is missing too. I can feel the thrum of something which might be unstoppable. My husband is talking quietly now about other things, about a book he has been reading which he thinks I will like, about a dog he sees when he goes for a walk. I go out of the bar and back into the reception area. I do not want to but my body takes me there. Through the phone, beneath the sound of my husband's voice, there is a ringing, a low, nearly silent tone, deep. In the reception I look behind the desk and there is, yes, a door, a red door.

THE PRIEST

I was in a film in the seventies which has become something of a cult classic. In the film I play a young country priest who has fallen out of love with God and is drinking in secret and waking up in the fields, wet with dew, not knowing how he got there. You can watch my audition tapes. They originally wanted a man for the role but I dressed myself up, and though I wasn't good, there was something about me that was right, maybe it was desperation. They bound my chest and I'm on lists now of the best queer characters of all time and the LGBTQI films to watch before you die. I wasn't pretending to be a man. I don't think I was really pretending at all. I cut my hair short and they slicked it back with grease and I got thin for the role by accident because I kept forgetting to eat.

When the film starts the screen is black for two minutes and there is a sound which begins quietly and grows louder and louder. I've sat in dark cinemas and dank sitting rooms and watched the audience as they move and shift uncomfortably and as the sound rises they grow still and it is the sound, yes, it is the sound of trees falling, yes, of one tree falling which brings the others around it down.

*

THE HOTEL

The film is a horror film. The director was a nobody but they'd got a big name to play the mother character and everybody thought it was going to be a hit. We were all drinking and partying but also working hard, up all night and then awake again in the early morning, take after take. We were ecstatic, the film was good and we knew it, but our marriages broke down, we all drank ourselves miserable, a lot of us would never work again. In the film I am passed out in a field and one of the other priests comes and finds me and leads me to the hotel where a girl has taken sick and might die. The hotel has long winding corridors with red carpets and blank windows. The girl is sick in bed and I stay with her and her mother through the night, which is long. There is something in the girl, something bad, and there is something in the hotel and as the night goes on there is something in me and in the mother too, we are bad, we are made bad, we are possessed or we have lost ourselves. Almost the whole film takes place in that one hotel room, number 63.

The Hotel was famous before the film for being spooky but afterwards it got really famous. Fans of the film went on pilgrimages to stay there, you could sleep in Room 63 where most of the film was shot, you could buy t-shirts with a photo of The Hotel on. After The Hotel burned down people would still go there, to visit the place it had been, to see if there was anything weird in the land, and there were stories online about what they found, crazed animals, words that came from the earth. I sometimes found myself wanting to go back there, really just wanting to get in the car and drive

The Priest

and drive until I came to that tree-lined place. I know why people get obsessed about The Hotel, go back there over and over. I get it.

Things kept going wrong on the shoot. A whole load of film was lost and we had to redo all the scenes; there was rot in the hotel room we originally used and the girl started coughing and we had to move to Room 63. We were all staying at The Hotel and I was sleeping with the woman who played the mother and I was trapped in these long, labyrinthine dreams in which I was lost and couldn't find my way out.

I'm going around and around what I have to tell you. I can taste my mouth the way it tasted that night. My hands were shaking and shaking because I hadn't had a drink yet and I kept getting lines wrong, stuttering. The child actress had never been in a film before and was a strange, quiet thing, like a lost kitten, with big staring eyes and a habit of popping up unannounced. After the film was over I kept trying to find out what happened to her and there were rumours she went mad or moved to Australia. After the woman who played the mother killed herself, the film got famous again because she was a big star and people started staying even more often at The Hotel. She'd been phoning and phoning me every night between three and four am but I didn't pick up because I knew that if I spoke to her I would remember what happened the night of the shoot in Room 63 – and then I wouldn't be able to go on living.

*

I suppose she wasn't able to go on living.

We were shooting some tricky scenes and the director cleared most of the set and I remember the smell of the room when we went in, like burnt onions. The girl was there already, made-up, in the bed, sickly looking, and the woman who was playing the mother was there too. In the scene the mother and I are in the bathroom, and when we come out we think the girl is dead, that she has died while we were in there, and then she wakes or comes back and there is a fight and I find God or I say I find God but God isn't there, he won't come, and the girl gets out of the bed and attacks the mother, tears a tooth from the mother's mouth with her hands. By the end of the scene there is blood on the floor and on the walls and it is a climax to the film, a moment beyond which there must be change.

The shoot was all wrong from the beginning. The night felt so heavy, clammy, resting on our faces and shoulders. In the bathroom the mirror was angled in a strange position and I kept catching awful sight of my face in it, my pocked skin, my sodden mouth. In the mirror the woman who was playing the mother was looking at me and mouthing something but when I turned my face towards her she was looking away. I understood – and this wasn't in the film, this was what I felt, so strongly – that there was more than one of each of us in the room, we were doubled and the mirror was showing our doubles. It took a lot of takes to get it right. I was sick in the sink for real and they kept that in, the sight of

The Priest

my face bent forward, the woman who played the mother sat on the edge of the bath in a dressing gown picking at her nails and watching me. The light is yellow and the walls are close and pulsing. After I am sick on the film the mother tells me about the things she wanted for her life and how sometimes she imagines the girl will die and then she will be able to do them. There is a meme of a line she says from this scene which I see all over the internet. In it she holds out her arms and says: I'LL BE THERE SOON. Over and over and over again.

In the film the girl is dead or she is not dead. The mother is on her knees on the floor howling without making any sound. I am trying to do CPR and I can see the girl's eyes moving under her lids. Then she opens her eyes and she reaches up and she puts her hands around my neck and she laughs and I am trying to get away from her because she is stronger than she should be. This is what happens in the film. The mother gets off the floor and says the girl's name over and over so that it doesn't really sound like a word anymore and she is trying to get the girl's hands off my neck and I am choking. I was choking, I realised. Not in the film but in real life. She was stronger than she had been before and her eyes were like dark spinning plates. I couldn't breathe. The mother was shouting and then the girl let go and got up on all fours like a small wolf and leapt at the mother and this was how it was supposed to be in the scene. She put her hands inside the mother's mouth and the mother was gurgling and this was how it was supposed to be and I was trying to help but I still couldn't breathe really and then I knew something had gone wrong because the mother's eyes were on me and I went to help and then there was blood, sprayed, and the girl was holding a tooth which was not the fake tooth but the woman who played the mother's real tooth and someone was shouting and shouting and I realised it was me. Then all the lights went out. They kept almost all of this in the film. There were lawsuits and big arguments but they kept it all in.

I know that when I die I will go to a place that is as dark as that room was dark. After the lights went out nothing was recorded. There were sounds of fumbling and things being knocked over and I stood very still and when I opened my mouth to speak I found that I couldn't, I was struck dumb. There were hands on my face, damp hands, and someone clambered up me and wrapped their arms around my shoulders and then began speaking into my ear, their mouth pressed against my ear. It was the girl. She talked and talked and I couldn't do anything but listen to her. She told me everything. She knew what was going to happen not just the next day or the next week but in years and years. She told me everything I would do in my life, every repetitious day, every stumbling morning, every mistake, every regret. And in the words there was something living that moved from her to me and is living in me now. I can feel it in my stomach, curled, shifting, living off me. The tears ran down my face but I couldn't move and then the lights came back on and the director was saying something and the girl was back in

The Priest

the bed, nodding sleepily, there was no blood on the floor or on my hands. The woman who played the mother was looking at me and I understood that she knew, that she had heard the way her life would go, that she had seen everything.

Sometimes I try to tell people what happened that night. I think it would be such a relief to say it out loud, to have someone else know. But, until now, I've never been able to. The words dry up or I find myself speaking about other things. I know, now that I've said it out loud, the words are in you too, inside you. I'm sorry. I'm sorry for giving them to you. I cannot take them back now. They belong to you just as much as they belong to me. Do you feel them? Can you feel them inside you?

THE FILM

This is the final story of The Hotel in the fens.

The film begins with a shot out of the window of a car. There's motorway, other cars going past, buses, lorries, scrubby trees, a service station, the reflection in the window of someone holding the camera, no face only arms extending. Someone off-screen says, here we go, here we go.

What it is not possible to see in the camera is that the car smells of the Subway sandwiches they have just eaten and the petrol Sian spilled on her shoes; it is not possible to feel the air conditioning which is very cold and difficult to control and the roughness of the seats beneath their arms and legs which feel heavy and hard to manoeuvre.

The film is unedited so what follows is a series of quick flashes of the journey, the car and their voices, the back of Sian's head as she drives, Karen's wide grinning mouth as she turns to look at the camera, Kelly's knees, someone's hand – nails painted aquamarine – on the radio dial, someone's voice lying to their parents on the telephone. Out of the front window the narrowing of the roads, the scissor away from motorway, the crackle of low branches over the roof. Where are we going? Where are we going? one of them chants and then Kelly's face is there, the camera turned towards her, held close. We're going to The Hotel, she says.

After they are gone there is less left behind than you would have thought. The film makes its way online, social media sites and then deeper: blog posts, the dark web. Their faces are there like stars that are already dead but still throw out some light, their words somehow vastly meaningful in a way they must never have meant them to be. What is left behind also, of course, are the gathered accoutrements of lives somehow made accidentally significant. The bare mattress in Kelly's student room with the dirty sheets balled at the foot, the scattering of crisp packets beneath the bed, a wad of money folded into the sock drawer. The window left open in Sian's house and the rain which had come in and stained the floor, a mark almost like a handprint. The smell of the bin in Karen's bedroom which she had not emptied and was moulding, rank. The emails they sent in the days before the film, curt replies to long family messages, pleading requests for essay extensions to professors. The milk half-drunk on their shelf in the fridge, the unanswered phone calls from partners or friends.

The Hotel first appears on the video as a smudge, ashy, through the window of the car. The suggestion of a building which then comes and goes through the trees, the sound of their excited exclamations, the shaking lens of the camera

The Film

picking it up and then losing it again. Seen properly The Hotel is unassuming; the chain-link fence around the outside, the boarded-up windows, the ground beneath scattered with broken roof tiles. There are ten or more long ashy chimneys left on the roof which is still standing, a wide white circle of damaged stone steps leading to the front door which is padlocked. The garden has grown wild, the earth is sodden, trees tangle together, the stone walls are crusted with ivy and other trailing plants. The three of them roam, looking for entrance, and occasionally it is possible to see inside through cracks in broken windows or rotten doors, the probability of rooms, darkened. They talk over one another so that most of the words are lost, but when they finally come to the window – not boarded, the glass broken – it is quiet and the camera is switched off so there is no video of them going in, nor any way of knowing what it might have felt like to clamber one after the other onto the rotting sill, and drop into the cold beyond; the smell, the sound of their own breath, their voices hushed in a sort of reverence.

From research on their computers, Word documents, email threads between the three of them, it appears they knew most of The Hotel's history when they planned to go there. In one particular email Sian writes that they should type up their conversations, try to collate their findings so that when the film is done they can show why they went, what they were looking for, what they hoped to find. The following emails are a mess of back and forth, crossing and recrossing the same thought, repetition of stories they have heard.

Often the emails come late at night and refer to a meeting the three of them have just had, an earlier discussion, a moment of revelation which they circle around. They are going to The Hotel because, of everywhere they have researched, it has the most troubling history. They are going to The Hotel because it was the last place Sian's mother was seen. The internet is ripe with warnings about The Hotel but still people visit over and over, return again and again. Throughout these warnings there is a suggestion that this pull does not only last in life but goes on through death. Put simply: they are looking to catch on film a place that is haunted. This is a description they are scathing of. They are looking to catch on film the uncertain, the uncanny, the marks of something other, a sign of ghostly repetition, of the hidden. What is left out here are the sentences buried beneath other sentences, the words hidden from sight. Rarely do they say: I am afraid of what we will find. Although they are. The sleep app which Karen uses shows that she is sleeping barely three hours a night by the time they leave; the messages Kelly sends her girlfriend are often troubled, anxious. In some of the emails Sian writes to them about her own history of The Hotel, her mother who worked there as a night porter when she was a child and who left or went missing.

They are inside now. There must be a torch strapped to the top of the camera because as it moves so does the light, pooling and fidgeting at the edges of objects, fallen chairs, ajar doors, smashed bottles. The light picking up, also, the forms of the other two moving cautiously ahead, bending now and

The Film

again to get a closer look at something, the light from their own torches occasionally swinging so that the camera is blinded by white. As they go Sian narrates falteringly what they are seeing: the ceiling collapsed in some spots so that, peering up, the camera makes out tangles of electrical wire pulled loose, the edges of other rooms above; in some places the furniture piled up as if in preparation for a bonfire. As they approach the stairs (in the emails it is always clear that where they were going was Room 63 and that they should make their way there as quickly as possible), Karen starts talking about what they might see, about what they might find. Sian interjects, disagrees. The camera is moving forward, the torchlight loping ahead up the stairs which are broken entirely in places, treacherous, curving around; now dancing, picking up hands, raised arms, a face turned back, the sodden mould on a once-white wall, their voices wavering closer and then further away, the first corridor lengthening with open and closed doorways leading off. In the camera something moves – something they do not see – a figure, there, looking out of one of the doorways they pass, and then gone. This is the beginning. This is the beginning of it being possible to know what is coming. That they will make their way to Room 63. That they were always going to make their way to Room 63.

Up the stairs, along the next corridor, up again and along. Looking occasionally into rooms but mostly picking up speed now, the camera sometimes showing nothing but Kelly's feet across the floor. Moments of strangeness which they see too, or which only the camera picks up: Sian or Karen appearing in one spot, smiling, looking back, and then a moment later in another; Sian appearing to fall ahead and cry out in pain and a moment later be standing there looking unsure, as if nothing has happened. The doorway to the sixth floor is on the ground, smashed down. In the recording they move in and out of sight and their voices come from different places, folding around, the words sometimes very loud and clear as if they are speaking directly into the microphone. Kelly counts the door numbers down quietly but number 63 is missing or they do not find it and have to backtrack and try again, coming upon it this time, the door open, the torchlight catching the wonky nailed-up numbers, the sound of Karen speaking their names inside the room although she is not inside, she is there, beside them.

What cannot be made out in the recording is the smell of their fear-sweat and the stench of the hotel around them and the floorboards which seem about to give way beneath their feet and the feel of the walls when they reach out to touch them, gritty with earth. What cannot be made out in the recording is the dead who have come back to The Hotel and who cluster close, trying to touch them.

They are in the room although there is no footage of how they got in there. The walls of the room are completely black with mould and the camera moves jerkily making it difficult to make anything out. Mayhem, a breakdown in vision, their faces, their faces, someone's hands covering the view, Sian is

The Film

crying and crying and she says, what are you doing here, what are you doing here? Karen says, Sian, stop it you're hurting me. The camera is in the bathroom which is better preserved than the rest of The Hotel and there are words on the walls: BE THERE SOON. The camera is spinning and spinning. Someone says: It's on fire, it's on fire now.

For six months after they go missing their parents – and Sian's grandmother – appear on the news asking for them to come home. In the shape of their faces it is easy to make out their children: Sian's nose, Karen's eyebrows, Kelly's stubborn jawline. They ask for information and also for the girls to come back, promise that they aren't in trouble. It is presumed that they have left of their own free will, frightened after inadvertently setting The Hotel on fire. There is footage of the burnt grounds of The Hotel busy with firefighters and afterwards, when it is empty and blackened. The footage of the film is not released but somehow makes it online and is watched by groups of teenagers in dark basements or by the girls' parents and friends. Their teachers. By sceptics and believers. Sometimes Kelly's mum will wake in the morning and find written on the notepad she keeps by the bed the words: BE THERE SOON. She has never been to The Hotel before but she will go there one day, she will go there soon.

Acknowledgements

This collection was originally written for Radio 4. My thanks to Justine Willett, who worked with me on these stories and produced and cast them so brilliantly. Thanks to all the extraordinary actors who performed them, especially to Maxine.

To everyone who works so hard representing and publishing my books at Jonathan Cape and Aitken Alexander, you know who you are, my enormous thanks.

Thanks, in particular, to Chris Wellbelove.

To my family and friends.

To Matt, as always. To our children.